VICTORY IN THE VALLEY

By Dickson Rial

Betty,
May the God of all comfort comfort your heart in the "homegoing" of your mate — Knowing that He is with the Lord and Victory is his —
Our love and prayers,
Dickson and Shirley

Dickson H. Rial © Copyright 2010

All rights reserved

No parts of this publication may be reproduced, stored in a retrieval system, or transmitted in any form or by any means, electronic, mechanical, photocopying, recording or otherwise without the prior permission of the copyright owner.

ISBN 978-1-4507-0199-0

Victory In The Valley

First Edition published 2010
by
Lulupress.com / Lulu ID: 7454790

Printed on Acid-Free Paper

THE 23^(RD) PSALM, A PSALM OF DAVID

1 The Lord is my Shepherd; I shall not want.

2 He maketh me to lie down in green pastures; He leadeth me beside still waters.

3 He restoreth my soul; He leadeth me in the paths of righteousness for His name's sake.

4 Yea, though I walk through the valley of the shadow of death, I will fear no evil, for Thou art with me; Thy rod and Thy staff they comfort me.

5 Thou preparest a table before me in the presence of mine enemies; Thou anointest my head with oil; My cup runneth over.

6 Surely goodness and mercy shall follow me all the days of my life, and I will dwell in the house of the Lord forever.

TABLE OF CONTENTS

DEDICATION
ACKNOWLEDGEMENTS
FORWARD

I	THE PREPARATION (INTRODUCTION)	Page 17
II	THE PREDICTION (Verse 1)	Page 25
III.	THE PRESERVATION (Verse 2)	Page 31
IV.	THE PEACE (Verse 2)	Page 39
V.	THE PRIVILEGE (Verse 2)	Page 47
VI.	THE PATHWAY (Verse 3)	Page 55
VII.	THE PRESENCE (Verse 4)	Page 67
VIII.	THE PROTECTION (Verse 4)	Page 79
IX.	THE PERIL (Verse 5)	Page 87
X.	THE POWER (Verse 5)	Page 93
XI.	THE PROVISION (Verse 5)	Page 99
XII.	THE PERMANENCY (Verse 6)	Page 103
XIII.	THE PROSPECT (Verse 6)	Page 109

DEDICATION

Roxie Slocum Morgan

"I thank my God upon every remembrance of you."
- Philippians 1:3

It is to our dear **Roxie Morgan** that I wish to dedicate this book. She found the Shepherd in her valley, which led her to a new and stronger commitment as a Christian.

Several years ago, Roxie lost her devoted husband, Norris Morgan, to illness. Never in my ministry have I witnessed a wife vigil for thirteen months at her husband's bedside in the hospital. She lived in that hospital with Norris and never left his side. It was during this time that not only did she meet Jesus in those difficult hours, but we all witnessed Norris finding a deeper relationship with his shepherd as well.

Roxie is more than a friend – she is family. She has made a difference in many people's lives as they have traveled through their valleys, as she has encouraged, given, prayed, and been their sister in Christ. We are grateful for the life and ministry of Roxie Morgan.

ACKNOWLEDGEMENTS

I would like to acknowledge with great thanksgiving and great gratitude so many wonderful, exciting people who have helped make this book a reality. They have been a lift and a joy to know.

First and foremost, I want to thank my Lord and Savior Jesus Christ for being my shepherd, and for calling me into this beautiful, wonderful ministry, of which I have been a part now for these 59 years. My Lord has never left my side through all the storms and the valleys that I have had the privilege to go through. I love Him so much for allowing me in these years to walk as a shepherd - and yet I'm still learning from Him Who called me into this work.

I want to acknowledge the encouragement of my wife, Shirley, and express my thanks for her unwavering loyalty, compassion, and understanding. We have walked down this road together for more than 48 years. I have never had to travel as a shepherd alone. The journey hasn't been nearly as difficult as it could have been. I've had Shirley by my side. She is always showing me by her life and her words of wisdom what an example she is to all. She has encouraged me to be a much better shepherd than I probably would have ever been without her love and support. Shirley has taught me more about God through her every day living, through her love for people, her tremendous abilities, and especially through the last 50 plus years teaching women the word of God. I have never found one like her. She has given me strength to go on.

Dawn L. Wills, once my personal administrative assistant, has given her every talent to see this volume, as well as others, become a reality. Their publishing could not have been completed without her loyalty and creativity. She is not just a typist or a super-secretary. I believe she could have written this book herself. She not only typed and edited the original manuscript, but she provided the creative assistance that we needed to experience the joyful completion of this project. I've never seen anyone with as many talents and gifts; she poured her all into this book, and I thank her from my heart.

I wish to thank my staff here at Orchard Hills Baptist Church – Shane Pruitt, our Associate Pastor, Steve Webb, our Minister of Worship, and Jake Tubbs, Minister of Youth, and Gonzalo Lopez, Pastor of our Spanish mission congregation. They are the finest you will find anywhere. They "make it happen" in our personal Jerusalem. I want to thank these faithful gentlemen, for standing by my side and for ministering as true shepherds. No church has a finer staff. They have become true servants, ministers, shepherds, and eternal optimists, seeing a rainbow in a rainstorm. They have helped me to learn to look for the silver lining.

To my children, Randy and Renee – they are the greatest blessings to happen to my life. It is my prayer that they never cease to follow the Shepherd through their own valleys of their lives. I am so grateful for their love and understanding over these many ministry years. They have certainly brought joy and encouragement to my heart. They are simply the best!

FORWARD

This book on the 23rd Psalm is the latest book written by my beloved pastor, Dickson Rial. He is a pastor, evangelist, author, bible scholar, educator, expositor, and my very dear friend since our first revival together in 1967. Knowing that Dickson has many articulate, prestigious and influential friends who could very well prepare a wonderful *forward* to this informative and inspirational book, I count it an honor and a great privilege to be asked to do so. After reading the manuscript of this book, it seems like the author wrote it just for me.

You probably will feel the same after reading *Victory In the Valley*. Since the author of this book knows me personally so well, I believe he had me write the Forward to make sure I read the book! He knows I needed it! He knows my ups and downs, and that most of my life has been spent in the valley. Dickson's keen insight into scripture has shown me that the valley is where the victories are won. I do not have to be struggling to reach the mountaintop, nor do I need to feel guilty because I did not make it. Praise the Lord! The real mountaintop experiences of life are found in the valley.

Do you feel worn out, tired, even burned out at times? Then this book is for you. Do you feel like you are always surrounded by some kind of storm with pressure to succeed? Then this book is for you. Do you have a nagging, uncomfortable feeling sometimes or that you are not as close to the Lord as you used to be? Do you sometimes feel you are not filled with the Holy Spirit? This book is for you. Do you allow your enemies to give you a negative attitude sometimes? Are there times in your life you feel like you are always in a struggle to reach the mountaintop? Do you need more time in the valley with the Shepherd? Then this book is for you.

This marvelous book has taught me that the Shepherd is in the valley. I feel much better about myself, and my relationship with the Lord now that I know I do not need to be trying to climb a man-made mountain for a man-made reward or experience. In the valley with the Shepherd is where I want to be. That is where all my physical and spiritual needs are met.

> Dr. Charles Massegee, Evangelist

CHAPTER I: THE PREPARATION

The 23rd Psalm is probably one of the most read, most appreciated portions in the entire Bible. Though written by David some 3,000 years ago, this short poem has never been improved upon or surpassed in any language. To our day, it remains the sweet, singing nightingale of the soul - the majestic hope among the trees of faith. What Handel's Messiah is to music, and Hahn's "Light of the World" is to art, the 23rd Psalm is to mankind.

Henry Ward Beecher wrote this of the 23rd Psalm: "It has filled the air of the world with joy greater than the heart can conceive. It has charmed more griefs to rest than all of the philosophies of the world. It has comforted the hearts of the poor. It has sung courage to the army of the disappointed."

The remarkable thing about the 23rd Psalm is that it is everybody's psalm. The little child learns it at his mother's knee, the youth seeks its wisdom in hours of temptation and uncertainty, the aged quotes it with quivering lips as the Angel of Death approaches. During all of the years from childhood to old age, it is quoted repeatedly. Why? Because of the comfort and encouragement and strength it gives to all mankind.

Not only is the 23rd Psalm everybody's psalm, but it meets everybody's need. Whatever the urgency or necessity, this psalm assures us that if the Lord is our shepherd, He will undertake. If I am discouraged and depressed, He provides rest and refreshment. "He maketh me to lie down in green pastures. He leads me beside the still waters." If I have committed sin, and all of us do, and lost the joy of blessed fellowship with Him, if I confess, His mercy will provide sufficiently. "He restoreth my soul." Does the future with its uncertainties confuse and perplex me? If so, I have surely forgotten all about His shepherding care. "He leads me in the paths of righteousness for His namesake." It could be that I am afraid of death and life beyond the grave. What little faith, yet he says, "Though I walk through the valley of the shadow of death, I will fear no evil, for Thou art with me. Thy rod and Thy staff, they comfort me."

Do I become disturbed by those who, because of hate, seek to injure me by their deceitful tricks and unkind words? Why should I? He'll not forsake me. "Thou preparest a table before me in the presence of my enemies." Is there a sense of weakness and fruitfulness as I try to be a faithful witness for the Lord? There are no limits to His power. "Thou anointest my head with oil." Do I complain and grumble because of an envious heart? I must take time to count my blessings. "My cup runneth over." Do I look to failing self and because of my own unworthiness, do I doubt my salvation and assurance of heaven? I need a greater vision of Him and less of myself. "Surely goodness and mercy shall follow me all the days of my life, and I will dwell in the house of the Lord forever." Praise God that in Him, every need is met. The 23rd Psalm tells me so.

It's interesting to note that there isn't a single petition in the psalm. It is a catalog of the mercies of God. Not once does the psalmist ask or beg for anything. He rejoices repeatedly in God's gracious and abundant provision. He says triumphantly, "The Lord is my shepherd. I shall not want." David knew all about the peaceful and happy contentment known only to those who thoroughly trust in the Lord.

I'm sure it is possible, unlike myself, that on occasions you have read the 23rd Psalm many times, and yet you may not have entered into the fullness of its meaning. Possibly, you have memorized it, but you don't know it by heart. Possibly you have quoted it, but you do not know it by experience. Have its divinely chosen words become a present reality in your life?

Before we go any further, we should acquaint ourselves with the preparation essential for the complete understanding of this passage. Consider what precedes and what follows the psalm. It is not by accident that the 23rd Psalm is between 22 and 24. Without experiencing the truth of the 22nd Psalm, it is impossible to appropriate the blessings of the 23rd. The 22nd Psalm is well known as "the psalm of a cross." In it, we see numerous prophecies of the agony of our Lord as He suffered upon the cross. The psalm begins with the question our Lord was heard to utter upon the cross: "My God, my God, why has Thou forsaken Me?" (Psalm 22:1) It ends with those solemn words: "He hath done this." – which may also be translated, "It is finished." Throughout the 22nd Psalm, we see the horrors of Mt. Calvary.

Now, look beyond the 23rd Psalm to the 24th. Read it through and what do you see? It is very, very clear. This is "the psalm of a king." There's no trace of a humiliated Savior, but rather the Man of Glory who turns to earth to rule and reign in righteousness. "Lift up your heads, o ye gates, and be ye lifted up ye everlasting doors, and the King of Glory shall come in. Who is this King of Glory? The Lord, strong and mighty. The Lord mighty in battle." (Psalm 24:7-8) As of yet, this has not been fulfilled, but indeed it will be when Christ returns to reveal His authority and power.

Now see the picture. Psalm 22 looks to the past, presenting the Good Shepherd as the Savior who was crucified for the sins of the world, proving His unlimited love for the world. Psalm 24 looks to the future, presenting a chief shepherd as the sovereign who will return for His coronation. On one side of the 23rd Psalm, we have Mt. Calvary; on the other side, Mt. Zion. Nestled between these two great mountains of revealed truth, we see the 23rd Psalm with its quiet, green valleys and still waters with the Great Shepherd gently and tenderly leading His sheep.

We are living in "folly days." The 23rd Psalm is for us today. It's a psalm of new life and resurrection glory. For all who believe in the Lord Jesus, the psalm may be a present reality. All the promises are for believers.

Before we go into any further study of this wonderful psalm, let there be no misunderstanding about the gate of entry. It is impossible to realize the joy of the 23rd Psalm without first of all going through the 22nd. What do you mean? Just this - you have no right to the promises of the 23rd Psalm until you recognize the redeeming work of Christ in the 22nd. Realize what He did for you and believe on Him as your Living Lord. You can know Christ's gracious and shepherding care after you know Him as your Redeemer.

So you want to get to the 23rd Psalm without the 22nd? That's impossible. Before the shepherd can care for the sheep, He must possess the sheep. The Prophet Isaiah tells us, "All we like sheep have gone astray. We have all gone our own way, and the Lord laid on Him the iniquity of us all." (Isaiah 53:6)

Because of our sins, we have shut ourselves out from the fold of God. But the way into the fold has been provided. The Lord Jesus IS the way. "The Lord laid on Him the iniquity of us all." Christ died on the cross for our sins. Indeed, He is the Good Shepherd, of whom we read in John 10:11 – "The good shepherd giveth his life for his sheep." This is the truth of Psalm 22 – Christ crucified. In Psalm 23, we see Him as the Living Lord, and indeed He is. He rose from the dead and longs to save and keep all who believe on Him.

But, I repeat. It is absolutely impossible to receive the promises and blessings of God until you receive the sacrifice that Christ provided for your sins. God has always demanded a blood sacrifice for sin. From Genesis to Revelation, there is no scriptural truth more prominent than "salvation by blood." It began at the gates of Eden after Adam and Eve transgressed God's law. The Lord appeared in His mercy and slew the animals as a blood sacrifice for sin, and using the skins as a covering for Adam's and Eve's naked bodies. This is a type of the covering for sin provided by the shed blood of the Lord Jesus.

Later, we see Abel offer a blood sacrifice from "the firstlings of his flock." (Genesis 4:4) By this act of faith, God numbered him among the believers, according to Hebrews 11:4. "By faith, Abel offered unto God a more excellent sacrifice than Cain, by which he attained witness that he was righteous.

After many years later, because of sin and judgment that was upon the earth, mankind was destroyed by flood. The only ones remaining were Noah and his family in the ark. In Genesis 8:20, it states: "Then Noah built an altar unto the Lord and took of every clean beast and of the clean fowl, and offered burnt offerings upon the altar." That was the first thing they did after Noah and his family left the ark.

Again, sin prevailed. God laid an entire new foundation for the establishment of His kingdom on earth. By means of the divine call of Abraham and the miraculous birth of Isaac, a new people was chosen to witness for Him, but this was not without blood sacrifice. Abraham soon learned the meaning of this great truth as he willingly offered up Isaac. God provided a ram as a substitute, and Isaac, who was to die, symbolically rose from the dead, typical of the believer's resurrection and Christ. This, again, was not without blood sacrifice.

We might consider Israel's deliverance from Egyptian bondage by the blood of the Pascal Lamb, sprinkled on the doorframes or the sprinkling of the blood first upon the altar, and then on the Book of the Covenant. After that, it was sprinkled on the people at Sinai as Moses declared the "blood of the covenant." (Exodus 24:8)

I want to hasten on to the New Testament. Some think the message of the blood sacrifice for sin is for the Old Testament only. What does the Bible say? There are scores of verses that teach just the opposite. I would like to choose one instance from many. When John the Baptist saw Christ at the beginning of the Lord's earthly ministry, he made two declarations. They are most significant. First, he said, "Behold the Lamb of God that taketh away the sins of the world." (John 1:29) The Lord Jesus was the perfect fulfillment of the Old Testament sacrifices. He was to shed His blood for our sins. Second, John said that the Lord Jesus is "He that baptizes with the Holy Spirit." (John 1:33)

The baptism of the Holy Spirit has to do with the placing of the sinner into a vital union with the Lord, whereby he enters into the fellowship and enjoyment of the Living Christ - the truth of the 23rd Psalm.

But there must be no mistake. Before the second promise can be received, the first must be believed. Christ must be received into the life as the One who suffered, bled and died for our sins. Again, this is the truth of the 23rd Psalm. Christ must be seen as "the Lamb of God that taketh away the sins of the world."

Have you accepted the Lord Jesus as your sacrifice for sin? If not, do so now, and then enter into all of the joys of the wonderful 23rd Psalm. Let the Lord truly be your SHEPHERD.

Charles Coburn, the late actor, once was asked how he managed to keep the lines in a play fresh and alive after weeks and sometimes months of reciting them almost daily. He explained that occasionally the play would be shut down for a time. The cast, the director, the musicians and all of the production personnel and even the writer would come together and read the play as though they had never heard it before.

Familiar Bible passages tend to lose their zest as we quickly scan them. "Oh, I know that. I've heard that all my life." However, when we apply Coburn's technique, the words become exciting again, as they stir the depths of our being. So, let us approach the 23rd Psalm as though we have never heard it before.

The psalm divides into three parts. First, David takes us into the glean. Then he takes us down into the gorge. Finally, he takes us on into the glory.

In the first part of the psalm, he introduces us to the one who can take care of our frailties. Then, to one who can take care of our foes. Finally, to one who can take care of our future.

I think of all the ways that we can divide this psalm. I like the best one that I found in my mother's open Bible there beside her bed. The day after she died, along side Psalm 23, I found that she had written: "The secret of a happy life, a happy death and a happy eternity."

CHAPTER II: <u>THE PREDICTION</u>

Verse 1 – *"I shall not want."*

In the first verse, David makes a startling prediction concerning himself and his future, saying, "I shall not want." The more I think about this, the more I am convinced that this is truly an amazing statement, for David was not only thinking of a day, a week or a month – yes, even a year – but, he actually meant "I shall never want."

You may be thinking, "How could he be so positive?" Well, that's very simple. David was a wealthy man. He was wealthy in his old age, but he offers no hint that his wealth provided such confidence. In fact, it was just the opposite. In Psalm 62:10, he eludes to the insincerity and uncertainty of riches. Listen to what he says: "If riches increase, set not your heart upon them."

The question comes to your mind, after reading that statement, "How does anyone know what tomorrow will provide? What do we know about the future?" You see how ridiculous this could be? But, when you realize, however, what precedes the phrase, there could be no question as to its feasibility. David's assurance that every need of his life would be supplied was not hinging upon his abundance or his riches, or the greatness of his power or his ability to achieve, but solely upon the principle that he belonged to the Lord. Listen to it again: "The Lord is my shepherd." Because of this realistic relationship with God, David could say with boldness, "I shall not want."

How marvelous it is to know that, in a world of confusion and darkness, the true believer in the Lord Jesus Christ can say, "I shall not want." You might remember that

Paul said in Romans 8:32, "He that spare not His own son, but delivered Him up for us all, how shall He not with Him also freely give us all things?" God is to be trusted not for <u>some</u> things, but for <u>all</u> things. Listen to what Job cried out to the Lord in Job 42:2: "I know that Thou canst do everything." You see, you couldn't throw Job off the track. He says in Job 13:15, "Though he slay me, yet will I trust in Him."

Many believers talk about trusting the Lord, but few seem to practice it. They trust God while all is well, but when adversity and troubles come, their faith disappears. They begin to worry and fret and complain, looking in every direction but UP. How foolish! God tells us that in Matthew 6:34: "Take, therefore, no thought for tomorrow for tomorrow shall take thought for the things of itself."

Has worry ever accomplished anything for you? I've heard of someone who said he did find worry to be an advantage; in fact, the things he worried about never happened. Doubtless, this could be said of most of our worries. But, actually worry in the believer is the denial of faith. There are no limits to God's ability to undertake for every occasion. He has promised to care for all the needs of our lives. Do you remember what Paul said in Philippians 4:19? "My God shall supply all of your needs." That means spiritual, mental, physical or financial – whatever they may be "according to His riches in glory by Christ Jesus." There are absolutely no boundaries to the scope of God's possessions. For this reason, He can fulfill all His promises.

Here's a lesson that we need to learn. When we realize fully God's abundance, we must trust Him wholeheartedly. An example of this: a sheep trusts the shepherd, so believers are to rely upon God. We are told that even before they are in the fold for the night, sheep know their shepherd has already planned for their grazing throughout the next day. They are confident that he will lead them to the green pastures. How and where, they do not know, but they have learned from past experience that his gracious care has always been for their well-being. They never worry, so why should we? Has there ever been a single occasion in your past when God in His love and mercy failed you? Why then do you worry? Take God at His word. Listen to what Psalm 37:4-5 says: "Delight thyself also in the Lord and He shall give thee the desires of thy heart. Commit thy way unto the Lord. Trust also in Him and He shall bring it to pass."

Sheep are the most helpless of all animals, and we are told that they are truly the dumbest. But, they know that they need not fear. With our burdened hearts and confused minds, we need to learn this simple truth. Paul tells us in II Corinthians 5:7, "Walk by faith and not by sight." Problems and worry will dim our vision. Like helpless sheep, we may not be able to see far ahead, but the shepherd is there. His eyes can see all things. Worry chokes the life of faith. Freedom from worry is faith in operation. If we have committed our life to Christ, and if He is our shepherd, we have nothing to fear.

ILLUSTRATION: Though sheep do have limited vision, God has compensated that by giving them an unbelievable sense of hearing. Their eyes may deceive them, but never their ears. Especially, they are sensitive to the shepherd's voice.

A writer tells of a traveler in Syria watching three shepherds whose sheep were being watered all mixed in together. The traveler wondered how the shepherds would ever get the sheep separated. One shepherd raised his hand to his mouth and called, "MEN-AH." This is the Arabic for "follow me." Immediately, thirty sheep clamored up the hill after him. Not one of his sheep remained.

Listen to what Jesus said in John 10:27: "My sheep hear my voice. I know them and they follow me." We may not see ahead, but we can hear His voice. That is, though, if we take time to listen. "Hurry", like "worry," is the result of unbelief and failure to trust God. Those who rush madly through the day without taking time to wait on the Lord with prayer and Bible-reading will not hear Him. They cannot possibly know His will. God promises in Psalm 32:8, "I will instruct thee and teach thee in the way that thou should go. I will guide thee with My eye." God sees all the perils and pitfalls up ahead. That's why He says, "Wait on the Lord, be of good courage, and He shall strengthen thy heart." (Psalm 27:14) Don't run ahead without Him. Take time to wait. He's never in a hurry. God takes His time. We, too, must take time to wait. Many of the failures and disappointments we have suffered are the results of haste. Do not rush. If we hear His voice and follow Him, the result will be that every need will be met. Worry will be unknown.

I believe that all worry in the believer's life is the failure to accept fully the first part of Psalm 23:1: "The Lord is my shepherd." But some would say, "Preacher, I believe on Christ, though I still worry." You have believed on Christ, but He is truly your Shepherd. He is leading your life and are you following? Remember – the shepherd always leads his flock. In the morning when he calls them from the fold, he leads them throughout the day and always stays before them.

ILLUSTRATION: There was a guide some years ago in Palestine who told his party of tourists that the shepherd always leads his flock. Later in the day, they saw a flock of sheep with a man behind, driving them. One of the party said to the guide, "I thought you said that this was never done?" "Correct," replied the guide. "Let's inquire." Going to the man, the guide asked why he as a shepherd was driving his sheep.

"SHEPHERD?" He replied. "I'm not a SHEPHERD. I'M A BUTCHER, DRIVING THE SHEEP TO THE SLAUGHTER!"

You may be sure Christ will never "drive" you to do anything. He is a Shepherd who lovingly leads His sheep. He says in John 10:4, "And when He putteth forth His own sheep, He goeth before them and His sheep follow Him." Twice in the 23rd Psalm, David declares, "He leadeth me." Let's read between the lines; if God were leading, David must have, at this point in his life, been following. Indeed, he was. Everything had been fully committed to the Lord – home, family, health, finances, old age. Everything was in the hands of the Shepherd. No wonder David could say, "I shall not want." Until everything is wholly surrendered to the Lord Jesus, we cannot say, "I shall not want." If there are any wants in your life at this moment, it's possible there has not been a full commitment.

One time, a little girl was called on in Sunday school to quote Psalm 23:1. Standing, she said, "The Lord is my shepherd, that's all I want." The believer comes to the place where he can say without reservation, "The Lord is my shepherd." He will then know deliverance from stress and worry, for when we love Christ whole-heartedly, there remains nothing to worry about. Every need will be met.

Is the Lord Jesus truly the shepherd of your life? This should be your only concern. Jesus says in Matthew 6:33, "Seek ye first the kingdom of God and His righteousness, and all these things shall be added unto you." Put first things first and all else will find its proper place. When Christ is your shepherd, all of your wants will vanish. The poorest believer becomes unspeakably wealthy. God will provide.

For many years, George Mueller had been known for his unbelievable faith and untiring confidence in God. Years ago, he founded and directed a splendid orphanage in England. At times, there were insufficient funds to carry on, but the Lord always responded to the humble pleas of this wonderful, committed servant of God. One day, as Mr. Mueller sat down to breakfast with the children, he explained that they had no milk, but that they should go ahead and thank God for the milk because their heavenly Father knew their need and would provide. As they prayed and thanked God for what they had not yet received, someone knocked at the door. When the prayer was completed, Mr. Mueller answered and there stood a milkman, who explained that his milk wagon was broken down in front of their orphanage, and that it was necessary to dispose of the milk. He offered it all to the orphanage absolutely free.

God does supply if we are in right relationship with Him. He says in Psalm 34:9, "There is no want to them that fear Him." To "fear God" is to permit Him to direct in all things. David said in Psalm 37:25, as he approached his last years, "I have been young and now I am old, yet I have not seen the righteous forsaken nor his seed begging bread." God will never forsake the righteous.

Is Christ your shepherd? Have you invited Him to come into your life? If you have, then you will make the same prediction David made: "The Lord is my Shepherd, I shall not want."

CHAPTER III: THE PRESERVATION

Verse 2 – *"He maketh me to lie down in green pastures."*

The 23rd Psalm presents, in marked clarity, many of the ramifications of the Great Shepherd's preservation of His own. David says, in this great psalm, "He maketh me to lie down." "He leadeth me." "He restoreth my soul." "Thou preparest for me a table." "Thou anointest my head with oil." Ultimately, He takes me to "the house of the Lord forever." Our Great Shepherd never ignores His task nor forgets His responsibilities. He faithfully watches over all who belong to Him.

David made many mistakes. He was like us; he was human. On one occasion, he slipped and yielded to temptation of the flesh, and wandered far from God, but the Shepherd sought him out and brought him back. David confessed to the Lord and all was well again. Later, with a heart overflowing with gratitude and with new assurance of the Lord's sustaining grace, he prayed, "Thou art my hiding place. Thou shall preserve me from trouble. Thou shall compass me with the songs of deliverance." (Psalm 32:7)

ILLUSTRATION: The Oriental shepherd had many duties in caring for his flock, but one of his chief responsibilities each day was to take the sheep to a good pasture. Very early, before dawn at about four o'clock, he starts them out on the rough terrain, leading on throughout the morning to the richer, sweeter grass where they enjoy the best pasture of the day. By ten or eleven o'clock, they are well aware of the tremendous heat of the noon-day sun. So, it is time to rest. Sheep are not always ready to rest when they should, so the shepherds must make them lie down. He gently taps his leading sheep on the head. Quickly, they all respond and others follow. Here, under the shade of a great rock, are some bushes. The sheep rest in the soft, beautiful, lush grass. Unknown to them, they are being prepared for the long trail homeward, which often leads over dangerous and untried paths. The experienced shepherd can see far ahead, so he prepares the sheep with refreshing rest.

We are told, in God's word, to "rest in the Lord." (Psalm 37:7) – Like most foolish sheep, we are too busy to rest. We are so occupied with our work and pleasure that we have little time for rest. Remember – the Great Shepherd repeatedly calls to us, saying, "Come ye yourselves apart and rest awhile." (Mark 6:31) As usual, our ears are dull of hearing. We are madly rushing on to self-chosen pastures, fighting through and receiving very little nourishment. You know how the prophet describes us in Haggai 1:6? "You eat but you have not enough. You drink, but you are not filled with drink." In other words, our souls are famished; our bodies are tired; our nerves are on edge. We cannot continue for a long time under these circumstances. Our Great Shepherd is mindful of this. Because He has placed Himself to preserve His sheep, He must act. Soon He does. In His loving kindness, He "maketh us to lie down."

ILLUSTRATION: God makes us do some things even though we do not wish to do it because the Lord feels like we are too occupied with secondary things to hear His voice. When we feel the touch of the rod, then we feel the touch of His rod in a gentle, but firm rebuke. Even though we are busy serving Him and trying to lead others to Him, we are not excused from spending time with Him.

ILLUSTRATION: Too often we are running to meetings and sponsoring programs, while neglecting to spend time in quietness with the Lord. Remember how unproductive and unsatisfying to try to serve Christ without His presence and power. I have to admit – there is so much wasted energy in Christian circles because of so little time being spent seeking God's leading. We are so busy "DOING" that we have little time for "RESTING."

ILLUSTRATION: Someone said, "Vigorous souls are not usually found in tired bodies." God created all of us with physical limitations. To ignore them or to exceed them may mean sorrow.

ILLUSTRATION/QUOTATION: Dr. F.B. Meyer has written: "There must be pauses and parenthesis in all of our lives. The hand cannot ever be plowing its tolls. The brain cannot always be majoring on the trains of thought. The faculties and senses cannot always be on the strain. To work without rest is like over-winding a watch. The main spring snaps, the machinery stands still. There must be a pause frequently interposed in life's busiest rush wherein we can recuperate our nerves and find some new energy."

The soul cries for rest even louder than our bodies. So often the needs of the body are respected while the soul is rejected. The Bible reminds us that one day, the body will perish and disintegrate into dust, but the soul will never die. Jesus asks, in Matthew 8:36, 37, "For what shall it prophet a man if he should gain the whole world and lose his own soul, or what should a man give in exchange for his soul?" The soul must be brought in touch with Christ during life. There is no second chance beyond the grave. It is urgent that we believe on Christ now.

Without the Lord Jesus in a life, the soul is restless and totally ignorant of the peace of God. For those who have committed themselves to the Lord Jesus, soul demands more than rest. It needs food. The word "pasture," as used in the

Bible, means "food," as well as "rest." To be mature and strong Christians, we must have spiritual food. We need to feed upon the Living Bread. Jesus said in John 6:52, "I am the Living Bread, which came down from heaven. If any man eat of this bread, he shall live forever."

How do we feed upon Christ? We do it by spending time in the "green pastures" of His word in the Bible.

ILLUSTRATION: Jeremiah was in the habit of spending much time feeding his soul in the Word. He confessed, in Jeremiah 15:16: "Thy words were found. I did eat them. Thou word was unto me the joy and rejoicing of my heart." Again, the psalmist says in Psalm 119: 103, "How sweet are thy words unto my taste, yet sweeter than honey to my mouth."

ILLUSTRATION: One great preacher of yester-year, said, "Those of God's people who give the first hour of their day to prayer and meditate in the word are the ones that shall receive the greatest blessings and shall be most widely used in reaching others for the Lord.

Many of God's people are carelessly "running" when they ought to be "feeding" and "resting." In their failure to spend time with the Lord, searching the scriptures and listening to His voice, they are getting spiritually weaker. Now, to avoid disaster with his sheep, the shepherd must respond to his sheep. Many of us abuse the privilege and ability we have to lie down in the green pastures so if we don't, the Shepherd makes it compulsory. Many of us may not feel the need of spiritual rest, but remember we are only the sheep; the Lord Jesus is the Shepherd. There are many things the sheep do not know. The shepherd knows all things. He is mindful of my limitation and yours, and refuses to permit us to get too far from Him.

ILLUSTRATION: If we have strayed, it may be that we should feel the "gentle touch of His rod," and "light affliction, which is for a moment, but worketh for us a far more exceeding and eternal way to glory." (II Corinthians 4:17) Trials and afflictions should always prompt the believer to heart searching.

ILLUSTRATION: Some time ago, I remembered a Christian making this statement to me: "Why did God do this to me?" I said to them, "Let us not be so quick to judge God." So often we bring sorrow upon ourselves. God permits this to prevent us from wandering further. Remember and don't be too upset. The Lord's chastening is extremely beneficial to all of us, and really, there are no exceptions.

Is it not true that in the hour of trial we get closer to the Lord? We learn as never before what it means to "lie down in green pastures."

ILLUSTRATION: David analyzed this in Psalm 119:67 and 71 when he said, "Before I was afflicted, I went astray, but now I have kept Thy word. It is good for me that I have been afflicted, that I might learn Thy statutes." David really realized that his affliction was not brought on as a result of what he was doing, but what he was not doing. He had been neglecting to spend time with the Lord. When temptation came, he was too weak to resist.

Suppose we do not respond to the "gentle touch of the rod?" Will our Great Shepherd forsake us in disgust and permit us to choose our own paths? Oh, no. He cannot do this. We must read His promise that He made in Deuteronomy 31:6: "He will not fail thee nor forsake thee." You see, we are His possession. We belong to Him. The psalmist said, in Psalm 100:3, "We are His people and the sheep of His pasture."

What then will we do if we fail to obey Him? What will He do if we fail to obey Him? A lot of the epistles in Hebrews answer our question: "Whom the Lord loveth, He chastens and scourges every son whom He receives." (Hebrews 12:6) If we give no attention to our Lord's gentle persuasion, we may be compelled to "lie down" as the result of His firm rebuke. Never forget: even the severest chastening is not without His love. The trials of life are not to punish us, but to correct us that we might appreciate and appropriate all God has provided.

We must realize what Jeremiah found out in his own life. In Jeremiah 10:23, he said, "Oh, Lord, I know that the way of man is not in himself. It is not in man that walketh to direct his steps. We need to remind ourselves of this fact constantly. I think all of us forget so easily. It is when we forget that God must do something about it. It is absolutely true that the child of God who refuses or neglects to follow the leading and direction of the Great Shepherd cannot know real happiness. He may think he is happy, but he is missing God's best.

Now, there is a question that we need to consider and that many of us do not understand until we go more in depth into this passage. Why are the shepherds in Palestine so concerned that their sheep follow the shepherd to the pasture? Why not just let the sheep wander and graze at will? In Palestine, pasture-land is very scarce. The absence of fences and the scarcity of pasture make it necessary that every sheep belongs to a flock, and every flock has a shepherd. Remember this: it is the shepherd's responsibility and not sheep's to find good pasture. The sheep must depend entirely upon the wisdom of the shepherd to guide them.

In Ezekiel 34:14, the Lord says of His sheep, "I will feed them in a good pasture and in a fat pasture shall they feed." God knows where the "good pasture" can be found. We need to rely upon Him to lead us.

ILLUSTRATION: Child of God, you may be suffering under the arm of God's discipline at this moment. I'm not saying all suffering is the result of our failure to obey the revealed will of God, yet much of it is. Could it be that you are a believer in the Lord Jesus Christ even though He is your Great Shepherd? You have been seeking out your own pasture. You have been neglecting to spend time in the presence of the Lord, fellowshipping with Him and feeding upon His blessed word. Maybe you are like me – many times my soul is starving. As a result, we become defeated, miserable and unhappy Christians.

What do we need to do? Confess to God. Let's make it right with Him. May it not be necessary for Him to make you "lie down in green pastures." Let's submit, yield all to Him. Lie down at His feet willingly, then like rested, well-fed sheep, you will know contentment. You will be satisfied with Christ.

CHAPTER IV: THE PEACE

Verse 2 – "He leadeth me beside the still waters."

So often, between the hurry and the bustle of life, the believer in Christ finds himself being swept along in the busy rush of the world. Usually, our quiet time is being neglected. We fail to rest in the presence of God. So, sometimes our Great Shepherd, Jesus, must force us to take the necessary pause. "He <u>maketh</u> me to lie down in green pastures." Rarely does he compel us to do things, but occasionally he must. Rather than compulsion, His much-used principle seems to be attractive: "He leadeth me beside the still waters."

Throughout the scriptures, we read repeatedly of our Lord's faithfulness in leading us on in the way of blessings. Like most of us, they do not always follow. But, nevertheless, God showered upon us love, and continued to watch over us. In fact, David writes in Psalm 139:7-10, "Whether I shall go from my spirit or whether shall I flee from Thy presence, if I sin unto heaven, Thou are there. If I make my bed in hell, behold Thou art there. If I take the wings of the morning dwell in the undermost part of the sea, even Thy hand leadeth me and Thy right hand shall hold me." The Lord always proceeds His own throughout every experience of life. Rather there be joy or sorrow, health or sickness, prosperity or depression, He is there to guide and direct.

<u>THE BEST IS YET TO COME</u> - Even more astonishing is the fact that the best is yet to come. The Lord Jesus promises that, after this life is over and they are all safely is His visible presence, He will continue to lead. Listen to what Jesus says in Revelation 7:17: "For the Lamb, which in the midst of the throne, shall feed them and shall lead them unto living fountains of waters and God shall wipe away all tears from their eyes." It has been a joyous privilege to know the Lord and to feel His nearness as He has led through the strange paths of life. "The confidence He has given that there is an eternity of blessing to come when His disciples shall see Him face to face."

"STILL WATERS" – With a heart overflowing with praise, David says in the 23rd Psalm, "He leadeth me beside the still waters." The quote "still waters" suggests to me God's comforting and sustaining peace. David uses the expression from his own experiences as a shepherd. He had to lead his dry, thirsty sheep to a water brook for much-needed water. He well knew, as does any shepherd, that although the sheep may be extremely thirsty, they will not drink from swift-moving water. Streams that have strong currents frighten the sheep. They will only drink from "still waters," surrounded by quietness and tranquility.

THUS, IT IS NOT ONLY THE SHEPHERD'S RESPONSIBILITY TO LEAD HIS SHEEP TO WATER, BUT HE MUST PROVIDE THE PERFECT PEACE REQUIRED TO SLACK THEIR THIRST.

ILLUSTRATION: This is precisely what the Great Shepherd has done for His sheep, which were born in to the waters of sin and knew nothing of the waters of peace. There was plenty of water, but troubled and disturbed, it was unable to quench the spiritual thirst of sinful hearts. For centuries, helpless and condemned souls vainly sought to provide their own waters, disintegrating into further hopelessness. Listen to what Jeremiah says in Ch. 2:13: "For my people have committed two evils. They have forsaken me the fountain of living waters, and carved them out of cisterns and broken cisterns that can hold no water." This prophetic condition still exists. Spiritually thirsty, their souls vanished. Many continued to search for the satisfying water of life. We live in an age of nervousness, frustration, depression and fear because unbelieving men and women are content to drink from "broken cisterns that can hold no water."

ILLUSTRATION: Would you believe that Americans take about six billion sleeping pills each year, plus many more drugs? Many are gradually becoming addicted to the so-called "tranquilizing" drugs. Be sure – peace can never be found in pills or drugs. Peace is found "beside the still waters." We discover that the "still waters" through him who said, in John 7:37: "If any man thirst, let him come unto Me and drink." Again, in John 4:14, he says, "Whosoever drinketh the water that I give shall never thirst, but the water I shall give him shall be in him a well of water springing up into everlasting life." Here's the satisfying water of the Living Christ. Those who drink of this water will never thirst. We will know the peace of God that forever vanishes fear and restlessness.

THE GREAT LOVE FOR THE SHEEP – It's not always easy for the Oriental shepherd to find an adequate watering place for his sheep. Nor, was it easy for our Lord to provide the "still waters." He had to suffer and die on the cross to prepare the way. Prompted by his great love for his sheep, He willingly made the sacrifice. Because of the price He paid, we may now come and drink of the "still waters."

There are so many troubled minds and hearts in the world today because they have not believed on the Lord Jesus Christ. They might realize that the moment they believe on Him, they become the eternal possessors of His peace. We read in Romans 5:1 - "therefore, being justified by faith, we have peace with God through our Lord Jesus Christ." What a wealth of blessedness we have in these quotes. "We have peace with God." His wonderful peace is immediately possessed by all those who sincerely trust in Him. This kind of peace is unaffected by circumstances, unchanged by time, underlining all life experiences. However ruffled the surface may be, "peace with God through our Lord Jesus Christ" is ours for believing.

Jesus said, in John 14:27, "Peace I leave with you and peace I give unto you, not as the world giveth give I unto you." The world makes an offer of peace, but it is unreal. The world can only give temporary peace. Christ gives eternal peace. The world gives peace as a doctor gives anesthetic. Christ gives peace that is life, hope and strength. The peace of the world is merely on the surface. Christ gives heart peace.

Actually, the world doesn't give peace. It sells it. It demands lust, fleshly indulgence, and painful sinfulness in payment. The peace that Christ offers is bestowed as a free gift. "MY PEACE I, JESUS, GIVE TO YOU." The world's peace operates only in favorable and peaceful circumstances. Christ gives peace that is effectual under any circumstances.

TROUBLE AND MISERY WOULD DISAPPEAR – If millions throughout the world would turn to Christ and drink from the "still waters" of His peace, their trouble and misery would disappear immediately. Only in Christ do we find the strength and grace to face the trials of life peaceably. Without the Lord Jesus, we have knowledge, but not wisdom - house, but not homes – speed, but not direction – medicine, but not health. It is Christ who really makes life worth living.

ILLUSTRATION: Mental Illness. One of the greatest enemies of our day that brings sadness to thousands is mental illness. Amidst the ever-moving tempo of modern life and because of the terrifying uncertainties of the future and the tragic drift toward extreme sinfulness, the minds of both old and young are being broken.

ILLUSTRATION: One governmental agency said, in 2002, that seven out of ten would need some type of psychiatric care at some time during their lifetime. The National Mental Health Foundation estimates that the figure would be higher by 2010. You ask, "Is there any solution for this pathetic loss of mental balance and health?" "Oh yes!" "THE PEACE OF GOD." Believe on Christ, follow Him to the "still waters," and you will find peace and rest for your soul.

PEACE WITH GOD – The Bible speaks about peace with God and the peace of God. The peace with God has to do with our relationship with Christ. The peace of God concerned our fellowship with Him. But, do not make "peace with God." All we need to do is receive it. Christ provided "peace with God" when He died on the cross and rose again for our sins. Believing on Him, we have "peace with God." As long as we do God's will and daily confess all known sin to Him, we enjoy His fellowship in the "peace of God." To persist in sin, failing to forsake it and to confess that sin, separates our fellowship with Him. Now, what is the difference? The "peace WITH God" remains, but not the "peace OF God." Let's go back to that sentence that "peace with God, which is **salvation**, remains but not the "peace OF God," which is **sanctification/fellowship.**

ILLUSTRATION: Suppose I entered a home where there are three small sons. Two of them are in the living room with their parents, but the third one is upstairs because of disobedience. The wayward child has not broken his family relationship. He is still just as much a member of the family as ever. What has he done? He has broken fellowship with his loved ones. He says that he's sorry and that he promises to do better. He remains separated from the family circle. So it is in Christ. If one believes, he enters into eternal relationship with

Christ, which can never be broken. He becomes a member of God's family, but by disobedience he may break fellowship with the Lord and lose the "peace of God." If there is repentance and confession to God, the believer is forgiven and fellowship is restored.

PRESENT REALITY – For the believer who is living in daily fellowship with the Lord, the assuring promises of Philippians 4:6 and 7 are always a "present reality." "Do not be anxious for anything, but prayer and earnest pleading, together with thanksgiving, let your requests be unreservedly made known in the presence of God."

The peace of God spoken about here is not something worked up, but poured in. It is supernatural, coming from God. It compensates for all our human limitations. No one can fully comprehend it. Indeed, it is far beyond intellectual analysis. We cannot describe its process, but we can certainly testify to its fact. It is real.

UNDERSTANDS EVERY SITUATION OF LIFE – Here is one reason why it's so real - given by Him who perfectly understands every situation of life: the Lord Jesus never learns about our troubles; He knows about them. Christians so not suffer alone. God suffers with them. He always goes before. "He leadeth me." What we suffer must first of all be endured by Him. A wise shepherd never permits his sheep to drink until he first tests the water himself. Our great shepherd has done the same. In Hebrews 4:15, He says, "He was in all points tempted like as we are, yet did not sin." He did not resist nor seek to escape. As a faithful shepherd, he drank of the poisonous waters that "He by the grace of God should taste death for every man." (Hebrews 2:9) He died that we might be eternally delivered from the penalty and the power of sin.

You may be going through a time in your life when it seems hopeless and useless to continue, but let me urge you – don't give up! Rest in the Lord. Drink of the "still waters." Our Lord understands. He knows what it is to be lonely and forsaken. Friends and even dearest loved ones turned their face from Him in the darkest hour of His life. He knows all about poverty, pain and disappointment. He realizes what it is to drink of the bitter cup of sorrow. He understands. To all the weary, He says, "Come unto Me, all you that labor and I will give you rest." (Matthew 11:28) There is PERFECT PEACE. There is perfect peace "BESIDE THE STILL WATERS" for all who will come to Christ and follow Him.

CHAPTER V: THE PRIVILEGE

Verse 2 – *"He restoreth my soul."*

In supplying the wants and needs of his sheep, the shepherd leads them to "green pastures" for rich nourishing food and rejuvenating rest. Next, he locates a brook with quiet and peaceful surroundings, where the sheep may enjoy refreshing drink without fear. Having rested, eaten and with their thirst quenched, they are now ready to journey homeward.

With such abundant provision, it might be thought that the dear sheep might never lead the watchful care of their shepherd, but occasionally, they did. Most of the roads they traveled were extremely narrow. The fields of grain of either side often proved to be too much of a temptation. One little nibble, and then another until deeper and deeper, the sheep would go into the fields – satisfying his hunger. Soon, he would be completely lost from the rest of the flock. Worst of all, he was lost from the shepherd's care. Usually, it was not long until the shepherd missed his sheep and would hastily start back and look for him. You can imagine how happy he would have been when he found the disobedient wanderer. Then, guess what happened. With this unusual affection, he "restored" the lost sheep to the flock.

ILLUSTRATION: When David said of his Lord, "He restoreth my soul," doubtless his thinking was reflecting back to the years of his youth when he, too, had sought out helpless sheep and restored them to the fold. Also, it probably prompted memories of his own failures in wandering from the Lord as a shameful king who had yielded to the lust of his flesh. For an entire year, David was completely separated from the joy of the Lord. Never had he been so miserable and unhappy in all of his life, but – praise God – he did not remain in that condition. He repented and came back. In the 51st Psalm, he tells the story. Listen to his pathetic cry as he was heartbroken by the bitterness of sin:

Psalm 51:12 – "RESTORE UNTO ME THE JOY OF THY SALVATION."

As He always does, God answered his earnest prayer. Restoration followed. Later, David compared the joy of fellowship with God with the emptiness of his superficial and sinful pleasures of the world. With a heart overflowing with gratitude, he voiced praise to the Lord. In fact, Psalm 16:7 says, "Thou will show me the path of life. In Thy presence there is fullness of joy; at Thy right hand, there are pleasures forevermore." David learned the hard way, but once and for all, he discovered that real happiness is found only in fellowship with God.

WANDERING FROM OUR LORD - All believers are like David in the respect that there are times when we, too, wander from our Lord's marvelous provision and care. What happens? Our hearts grow cold and we lose vision of the work that needs to be done. With little concern for the Gospel and lost souls, we live for ourselves. Indifference snuffs out the passion that once burned within us. We lose our "first love," and with it, the joy of our salvation.

It is easy to lose our spiritual fervor for Christ. We may be fiery hot for Him today, but icy-hot for Him tomorrow. I think the hymn writer of one of my favorite songs expressed our waywardness well when he wrote, "PRONE TO WANDER, LORD I FEEL IT. PRONE TO LEAVE THE LORD I LOVE."

SIN SO APPEALING - Considering our Great Shepherd's relentless provision of the "bread of life," the "living waters," and the "perfect peace," we might well wonder how anyone could forsake all of this for the pleasure of sin. But, we all do. Satan makes sin so appealing and so alluring. Not until after we have submitted to his shadow and deceitful claims do we find them to be ridiculous and foolish.

Satan lures us in many ways, but one of his well-worn ways is to try to keep Christians comfortable. "Seek your own comfort," he whispers in our ears, "and all will be well." Regretfully, we listen and believe him. We build bigger houses and cram them with all the latest gadgets. We accumulate and store up treasures for ourselves. Caught up in the thinking of the worldly-minded, we feel that security and happiness are found in "THINGS."

The Lord Jesus taught just the opposite. In Luke 12:15, it says, "Beware of covetousness for a man's life consists not in the abundance of things which he possesses." Let us not be deceived by "things." "Things" cannot produce happiness and lasting joy. Only Christ does that. Anyone who believes on Jesus receives this "great joy" as a gift. There is a danger, however, that we may strain from the Lord and lose NOT our salvation, but our JOY. Remember – this is not God's will for any of us. It tells us in John 15:11: "These things have I spoken unto you that my joy might remain in you and that your joy may be full." From this passage, it is so obvious that the Lord desires that we bathe in His joy every day of our lives.

THE LOSS OF THE GIFT OF JOY - How can we best guard against the loss of this marvelous gift of God's joy? One of the most elementary, yet important things we can do is spend time communing with Him in prayer. No matter how "material" we may be as Christians, none of us is strong enough to face the tempter alone. Remember what Paul said in I Corinthians 10:12. Let's heed his advice. "Wherefore let him that thinketh he standeth take heed lest he fall." Again, the psalmist says, in Psalm 124:8, "Our help is in the name of the Lord, who made heaven and earth." Remember that we are so weak and needy, but the Lord is strong and so sufficient. If we are going to enjoy His strength, it is mandatory that we carefully set apart a definite time each day – preferably first thing in the morning – to commune and fellowship with God in prayer. Others may want to be with Him late at night. Whatever is best for you…at least try to have a definite time to be with the Lord each day.

A TIME WITH THE SHEPHERD - It's interesting to note that each sheep had a time of quietness and aloneness with his shepherd every day. Early in the morning, the sheep would form a grazing line and keep the same position throughout the day. At some time along the way, each sheep would leave the grazing line and would go to the shepherd. The shepherd received the sheep with outstretched arms, speaking kindly to it. The sheep would rub against the shepherd's leg or, if the shepherd was seated, the shepherd would rub his cheek against his face. Meanwhile, the shepherd would gently pat the sheep, rubbing his nose and ears and scratching its chin. After a brief time of this intimate time together, the sheep returned to its place in the grazing line.

ILLUSTRATION: Even as the sheep had the need of communion with their shepherd each day, how much more important is it for us, who claim to love Christ, to recognize the importance of spending time with Him? If we truly are to follow the Lord Jesus, we must be men and women of prayer.

ILLUSTRATION: Have you ever noticed in the Bible how thankful Jesus was in communion with the Father? Yes, He was burdened with a busy ministry of healing the multitudes. He realized the necessity of withdrawing for prayer. Remember what happened when great multitudes came together to hear and be healed by Him of their infirmities? Many times, He would withdraw Himself into the wilderness and pray. Read Luke 5:15-16. Again, in Mark 1:35, there is something very striking, I think – "In the morning rising up a great while before day, He went out and departed into a solitary place, and there prayed." On another occasion, He went "out into a mountain to pray and continued all night to pray unto God." (Luke 6:12)

When Peter was about to be tested, Jesus said to him, "Simon, Simon. Behold, Satan had desired to have you that he might shift you as wheat, but I have prayed for thee that thy faith fail not. (Luke 22:31-32) Again, in John 14:6, Jesus tells the disciples He would pray unto the Father for the coming of another comforter, the Holy Spirit. You can never read the intercessory prayer of our Lord in John 17 without sensing His tireless concern for prayer. He prayed as He hung from the cross – "Father, forgive them for they know not what they do." (Luke 23:34) Just before He died, He prayed, "Father, into Thy hands I command my spirit." (Luke 23:46) As our risen and ascended Savior, He still prays at the right hand of the Father. You remember what Hebrews 7:25 says – "He ever liveth to make intercession."

If the Lord Jesus, who was sinless, gave Himself so unreservedly to the practice of prayer, how much more can we who are poor and weak and dependant creatures live without it? To all Christians, our Lord says, "Enter into thy closet and when thy shut thy door, pray to thy Father which is in secret and thy Father, which sees in secret, shall reward thee openly." (Matt. 6:6) Let nothing interfere with your quiet time with

God. If there is anything preventing this necessary fellowship with Christ, forsake and get rid of it immediately.

ILLUSTRATION: A businessman told his pastor he was so busy that he didn't have time to pray. The wise pastor replied,

"If you have so much business to attend that you have no time to pray, then you have more business on hand than God ever intended for you to have." I say, "Amen. Anything that hinders prayer in a believer's life does not belong in that life."

FAILURE TO COMMUNE - Failure to commune with God will make us easy marks for temptation to sin. When we are out of touch with God, anything can happen. The bars will be lowered and sin will find its way into our hearts. Spiritual things will become less and less interesting. Worldliness will be most appealing. With the loss of interest in Him, our joy we once had completely disappears.

Suppose someone has drifted into this backslidden state. Suppose the light of Christ in the heart has been clouded by sin. What can be done? The same thing David did – confess the sin to the Lord and repent, and then, with new-found joy, you will say as David, "He restoreth my soul."

OUT OF FELLOWSHIP WITH GOD - Are you out of fellowship with God? He desires that you and I come back. He will receive us. This is our privilege as a Christian. God knew how unstable and changeable we would be. He knew our weakness and provided in advance. Listen to I John 2:1-2: "My little children I write unto you that you sin not. If any man sin, we have an advocate with the Father, the Lord Jesus, the Righteous, and He is the propitiation for our sins." The Lord was crucified not only for some of our sins, but for all – past, present and future. Hallelujah!

Because of His complete sacrifice, immediate forgiveness and restoration is available to all believers. John further tells us, in I John 1:9, "If we confess our sins, He (God) is faithful and just to forgive us of our sins and to cleanse us from all unrighteousness." God will never refuse to forgive the repentant believer. He promises immediate forgiveness if we confess to Him. We are not to beg for forgiveness, but receive it on the grounds of Christ dying upon the cross. At the very instant, He forgives us, He restores us into fellowship and communion with Him.

Could it be that you and I have wandered away from love and mercy of our Great Shepherd? You and I are like wandering sheep. Some of us have strayed onto strange paths. In all probability, it began when you neglected prayers, or possibility you chose the wrong companions. Or, was it the practice of a secret sin that drew you away from Christ? It matters little which. The fact remains – if you come back to God, He will heal you and restore you.

ILLUSTRATION: There's always a tendency of just sinning against the Lord to run from Him and hide, as did Adam and Eve. "And lo, God came looking for them, calling, 'WHERE ART THOU?' How foolish they were. It was bad enough to sin and sever precious fellowship with the Lord, but to try to hide from Him was even worse, especially since it was not an angry God searching for Adam with a club – but a God of mercy, ready and willing to forgive.

Our present problem is not "where is Adam," but "WHERE ART THOU?" Are we in fellowship with Christ or is it true of you, as Isaiah declares in 59:2, "Your iniquities as separated between you and your God, your sins have hid His face from you that He will not hear. But, if you confess, He will hear and forgive."

Child of God, away from the Lord – come back to Him. You know you cannot have real joy out of fellowship with Christ. Get into the center of the will of God…confess your sin to Him and He will "restore" your soul.

CHAPTER VI: <u>**THE PATHWAY**</u>

Verse 3 – *"He leads me in the paths of righteousness for His namesake."*

INTRODUCTION: The inscription on a plaque on Florida's Singing Tower states: "I've come here to find myself. It is so easy to get lost in the world." True! Literally or figuratively speaking, getting on the wrong road is a frustrating, time-consuming experience. Staying on the right road of life can only be accomplished through following the Lord's direction.

He leads me in the paths of righteousness for His namesake. This verse could be rendered: **He leads me in the true paths for the sake of His name.** The International Critical Commentary presents it like this: ...in right tracks. Moffitt translates it: "He guides me by true paths, as He Himself is true." We would express it in this way: "He keeps me on the right track." David remembered his own experience as a shepherd. He knew that sheep had no sense of direction. Other animals do, but sheep do not. Even in the days of prosperous Roman rule, there were few good roads in Palestine. Most of them were winding footpaths about 20 inches wide. Confused travelers often lost their way because of the uncertainty of these paths. Some ended abruptly in a field. Others led to a waterway or a dangerous cliff. Obviously, it was a well-known impossibility for the sheep to go anywhere without the shepherd. You and I are no different.

The shepherd psalmist was saying that God guided by walking ahead of him on the right path. Left on their own, sheep tend to wander around and become lost easily. In fact, in the Middle East, the shepherd walks in front of the sheep. He makes sure that the paths are wide enough for all the sheep to follow comfortably.

UNDERSTANDING DIVINE GUIDANCE: The phrase, "He leads me in the right paths to uphold His name" is a possibility rendering. We of the Christian faith say that we believe in divine guidance. Now the secular world says, "You mean to tell me that God in Heaven speaks to you? Have you ever heard God speak audibly?"

This generation has difficulty understanding such truths for two basic reasons: magnitude and communication.

Mark Twain wrote that he did not believe God knows why we are here. The universe is too large for any person to fully comprehend.

ILLUSTRATION: According to a story, two men had the awesome adventure of being lost in space and landing on a distant planet. They found the natives friendly enough, but lacked in understanding.

"Where do you come from?" the natives asked.
"Why, we are from Earth, the men replied.
"Earth? What is that?" they asked.
"You know, the planet Earth," they answered.
 They proceeded the best that they could.
"Oh, yes, we know of that place. We call it the Wart."

Sunlight travels at 186,000 miles per second. It requires 50 million years for the light from a distant star to come into view. We are seeing light from a few stars that have already burned out. In a cosmos so vast, how can God be interested in whether I take that job, or whether I have personal problems or relationship?

DIVINE GUIDANCE IN COMMUNICATION - How can a people who do not adequately communicate with each other receive direction from God? As Christians, we declare firmly that God does guide us by faith. This truth is found in the total witness of the Bible. How, then, do we receive God's direction? How does He keep us on the right track? Our road map of the right path is the Bible. This Bible is salvation history. It is the Word of God. Through its pages we find the mind of God.

ILLUSTRATION: A fellow once explained how he found what God wanted him to do. He remarked to me rather impressively, "I just take my Bible, open it at random, and wherever my finger falls, God speaks."

I told him of another person who used the same method. He said, "Lord, speak to me, and put his finger on the verse. And Judas went out and hanged himself." (Matthew 27:5). This statement did not seem appropriate, and so he turned over several pages and read, "Go and do thou likewise." Luke 10:37.

Although this helter-skelter method is not adequate for guidance, we must never forget that the Word of God is the lamp unto the feet of the believer. Passages must be considered in context in the light of the total Biblical record.

Furthermore, there are times when God uses the fellowship of the church to reveal His will. I have seen numerous individuals discover answers through prayer within some group in the church. The message of God is in the hearts of His gathered community. A person shares his concern with Christian friends, and they combine their knowledge and prayer power. Thus, God makes His plans and purposes known.

WE ALSO RECEIVE DIRECTION BY USING OUR COMMON SENSE - One person remarked, "I prayed about a problem and never did get an answer, so I used my common sense and everything came out perfectly." God is a part of our common sense, too. He works in our reasoning process, or our common sense. He is inside of us already; we must let the Spirit break out.

GOD SPEAKS FROM WITHIN - Another way God speaks to us is in what the Quakers call INNER LIGHT. The truth comes to us from within. You remember what Samuel said in chapter 4:10: Samuel answered, 'Speak, Lord, for thy servant heareth.' We say, Listen, Lord, for thy servant speaketh. **We must learn to listen.**

ILLUSTRATION: A grade school teacher was having difficulty with her students. There were so many discipline problems that she could not challenge the children to reach their potential. One day, she had an idea. When the class began, she said, I want all of you boys and girls to bow your heads and see if God will say anything to you.

Thus, she started class day after day. Over a period of six months, the changes in the students were dramatic. The children reported what God said to them: God told me not to cheat on my math test and more. God said that I should mind my mother and daddy. God told me I should listen better in school.

The inner light is present. We must take time to listen. Remember Isaiah 40:31 says: They that wait upon the Lord shall renew their strength. They shall mount up with wings as eagles. They shall run and not be weary. They shall walk and not be faint.

There are times when we receive the wrong answer. A particular revelation or voice from God should be examined in conjunction with other ways of the Lord's guidance. Any light, which is contrary to Bible teaching, is false. God will **not** tell a person to do something that is in disobedience to His written word.

Browning was right: **Every brush is alive with God.** He is speaking, and we do not even know it. On occasion, the Lord breaks through in a special demonstration. There have been divine times in my own life when the only explanation for an experience was **God spoke to me.**

ILLUSTRATION: A little boy asked his mother if he could go out to play "catch with God." How in the world do you think you can play catch with God?" she asked in amazement.

"Well, that's easy", the boy replied. "I throw the ball up, and He throws it back."

We are reminded of Jesus' desire that we come to Him as little children. His plan for our lives becomes clear as we know Him more intimately.

ILLUSTRATION: A young girl in an orphanage was cared for by a man whom she did not know and had never seen. Every need had been met by this wonderful person. He showered her with gifts, even from distant places. He sent her beautiful dresses covered with lace and ribbons, and he provided, as well, her every day necessities. Through the years, this generous man exhibited his love and care without being recognized or known by the girl. Only once she saw his shadow, and for that moment, she called him _Daddy Long Legs_ because his shadow made him appear tall and lean. She finally met her _Daddy Long Legs_ and fell in love with him.

ILLUSTRATION: In Exodus 33, the account is given of another person who saw only the back of the One who gave him provision and direction. After the children of Israel had made the golden calf and had been disciplined because of their terrible deed, God told Moses that it was time to move on. The place of worship was out by the camp, and **those who sought the Lord** (Exodus 33:7) went to worship. Moses went out to talk with God. Then, he received assurance that God was going with them.

However, Moses wanted more. He wanted to see God's face. Since it is not possible for anyone to see God's face and live, God put Moses in a hole within a rock and covered the opening with His hand. After His glory passed by, God permitted Moses to see His back. From this experience of a renewed vision, this liberator moved forward with the people.

Rarely, do we see God when He moves through into our lives. Many times, we do not know that He is present in a precise moment. We, like Moses, see only the back of God. We know that He was present in the events of our lives only as we look back in our past experience. We must **never** forget - and, oh, how important this is - that through these years, we have been sustained by One who cares for us. He does not ever tire nor demand recognition. He simply gives to us from His treasures. Those who really know Him love Him.

ILLUSTRATION: All of us could learn a lesson from the Scot shepherd dog. If left to guard his master's coat, he will not leave it until the master returns. Nothing can draw him from the task to which he is appointed. Even though a rabbit may hop even under his nose, the obedient dog will not move. A deer might dart across the path and even so close that the dog could easily catch it, but the dog does not budge. I suppose that if the dog had a mind like some Christians, he might reason like this: "Certainly my master was unaware that a rabbit would pass by me so closely or that a deer would dart right in front of me. Surely he expects me to run after them." But, no, the Scot shepherd dog is faithful to his assigned task.

Those who are ready and willing to obey God's will are in a position to seek His leading. How may this be determined? There are three ways by which God speaks to us: 1) Bible reading, 2) Prayer, 3) Circumstances.

BIBLE READING - I have never known the Lord to lead anyone contrary to that which is written in the scriptures. It would be ridiculous for God to give us a book to live by and then direct us to do just the opposite. God speaks through His Word. In fact, James 1:5 says: "If any of you lack wisdom, let him ask of God and it shall be given him." Many times, this divine wisdom is found through the record reading of the Bible.

GOD ALSO SPEAKS TO US AS WE PRAY - Prayer can be communion. Never forget that communion is two-sided: not only do we speak in prayer, but we patiently listen.

We should converse with God, but we should also give Him the opportunity to speak. Usually, He is more willing to speak than impatient believers are willing to listen. Never forget this - real praying is not a hasty five-minute session in the morning or a sleep sentence in the evening. We are supposed to pray without ceasing, waiting on God.

CIRCUMSTANCE - We also determine the Lord's will through providential circumstances. We may be guided through a word spoken by a friend or a loved one, or by something said in a sermon, or by a line or two we might read in a book through the prompting of the indwelling Holy Spirit.

Thus, as we wait on God through the Bible reading, prayer and circumstances, we shall discover the mind of God. All three will be in harmony. One is not sufficient in itself for divine guidance. Someone has said this:

"BIBLE STUDY ALONE WITHOUT PRAYER WILL PRODUCE A PHARICEE. PRAYER ALONE WITHOUT A KNOWLEDGE OF GOD'S WORD WILL PRODUCE A FANATIC. USING CIRCUMSTANCES ALONE FOR GUIDANCE WITHOUT THE BIBLE AND PRAYER WILL PRODUCE A FATALIST. ALL THREE WORKING IN PERFECT UNITY WILL ENABLE US TO DISCERN THE LORD'S LEADING."

ILLUSTRATION: A family planned a picnic. The children insisted that all their friends and several neighbors be invited. The mother frantically gathered together their favorite treats and fried a large platter of chicken. Then, they went out and found a shady spot and opened the lunch. After eating the lunch, the adults sat around while the children went off to play. But, one dad warned, "Don't go past that fence. Play in this area. Don't cross the fence." What did the children do? You guessed it. They approached the fence with uttermost caution at first. Then, when no one was looking, over the fence they went. The older folks were deeply engaged in conversation by then and didn't seem to notice.

Things were even better on that side of the fence. Well, mom and dad didn't know anyhow. So, the children ran and played and found another fence, which they promptly jumped over. Several fences and hedges later, darkness fell around the children, and they had that sick, lost feeling. They called for their parents, but heard no answers. Then, they argued with one another about the right way to get back to the family.

That's our world today because it reminds all of us of that scene: individuals, groups, churches, countries wander off. They cross fences, traditions and principals and they rebel and disregard their ancestors' warnings. "Go this way," they say. "I'm not going to believe that. I'm going my own way." The road gets dark, and then a revelation comes. This path does not lead anywhere except into a dark swamp. They fight and argue concerning their next move.

THE RIGHT MOVE - Of course, after we have determined God's will, we must do it. John says in John 13:17: "If you know these things, happy are ye if ye do them." Happiness is not just merely **finding** knowledge of the will of God, but in the **doing** it. Many a life has drifted off into failure by refusing to do what God wanted. The greatest mistake in life is to say **no** to God.

When the compass was first introduced, it changed the limits of navigation. Up to that time, sailors kept their vessels close to shore. Why? They could use the stars for direction or for watching landmarks along the coastline. This device enabled ships to go through uncharted courses without any indicator outside the vessel. That is why the compass changed the world.

Jesus Christ gives inner guidance to those who let Him enter their lives and have control. Some of us are often like that executive who became lost every time he went hunting. His staff gave him a compass since they feared for his safety. The following Sunday, he went out again and got lost. As usual, the employees questioned him and asked him, "Didn't you take your compass? Oh, yes, he answered, but that thing didn't work. I started walking north, and the compass pointed southeast. It doesn't work."

We have the direction at hand, but choose to follow our own plan. Have you ever heard anybody say, "I've been reading my Bible and praying every day, but my life is all fouled up? – Or -- I've been following Jesus to the best of my ability, trying to live in freedom and joy in fellowship with

Him, and I've made so many bad decisions." His way works. Those who refute it have not experienced it for themselves.

CONCLUSION: In the book *I Will Lift Up My Eyes* by Glen Clark, he says in that book that for many years he wanted to write an inspirational book. Each time he tried, the pen would freeze in his hand. Then he heard another author, Marion McGraw, share her story. She also wanted to write but somehow she could not. In her dilemma, she discovered a little verse in the Psalms. It was Psalm 18:33: "He maketh my feet like hind's feet and set me upon my high places". She remarked that after she had received her hind's feet, the inspiration flowed.

Following the lecture, Clark rushed backstage to question this writer. What did she mean? What do hind's feet have to do with writing? But, she was gone.

Later Clark was on the verge of a nervous collapse. For therapy, he went to a ranch and worked as a cowhand. One morning, the foreman said, "Get your pony and ride with us. We're going into the hills to mesa No. 6 to take some salt to the cattle."

So, he rode with the cowboys up to mesa No. 1 and then to No. 2, and all the way to mesa No. 5. At this point, the foreman said, "Dr. Clark, you'll have to stay here. You can't reach the top of mesa No. 6."

"Why? Why can't I go along?"

"You see, the path is rocky and dangerous. Your horse doesn't track. Look, watch my horse." Then, he demonstrated. The front feet lift up and the back feet fall exactly where the front feet were. "My horse is sure-footed. He runs like a deer. Then, Clark remembered: He maketh my feet like hind's feet. Clark said, You go on. I have something to think about". He got down on his knees and prayed, "Lord, I should take off my shoes because this is holy ground. Forgive me for not following You. My life just doesn't track. My rhythm and coordination are gone. Make my feet like hind's feet."

Clark went home. The tug-of-war, which had been in his life, was not there anymore. He had the freedom to write.

At the end of a person's life, you may hear numerous statements about the deceased. "Mr. Smith left $50,000. Dr. Smith could pull teeth better than anyone in town. Mr. William was the shrewdest lawyer in the state. Mrs. Cantrell was the most competent teacher I knew. Mr. Walker played golf better than anyone else in the club."

I remember hearing a lady remark, "Isn't Mr. Bond wonderful? He knew every card in my hand last night at bridge." Then someone else replied, "Has it ever occurred to you that Mr. Bond is 45 years old and bridge is all he knows?"

Make sure the path leads you at least to the place where you want to be. A careful traveler will study the map before setting out.

"In all your ways, acknowledge Him, and He shall direct your path." (Proverbs 3:6)

CHAPTER VII: THE PRESENCE

Verse 4 – *"Yea, though I walk through the valley of the shadow of death, I will fear no evil, for Thou are with me."*

INTRODUCTION: A little girl was terrified by tunnels. She frequently traveled on a train with her family, and every time they approached a tunnel, she would press her face against her mother. The moment the train entered the tunnel, she would look only when she was assured they were once again out of in the sunshine.

A few years later, her fear completely disappeared. While driving along the Pennsylvania turnpike, the child was thrilled as they passed through the tunnels. Her mother, remembering the child's former fears, asked, "What made the difference?" The little girl replied, "Mother, I like tunnels because they have light at both ends."

This is a fact that God wants us to discover about all valleys, as well as all tunnels. If God is with us, there is light at both ends.

From a shepherd's perspective, this statement in verse 4 marks the halfway stage in the 23rd psalm. Up to this point, the shepherd has been on a home range, motioning to his neighbors about the excellent care he receives from his owner. In this verse, the shepherd turns not to his neighbor, but to the Shepherd directly. Notice the personal pronoun "Thou" enters the conversation.

Winter and spring have ended. As summer begins, the shepherd leaves the sheep to the high hill country. There, the grass is greener, the nourishment is plentiful and, during this period, the flock is in intimate contact with the shepherd and under his personal supervision – day and night.

Divinely chosen paths are always best for the child of God. There's no place for greater security or safety. They follow the Great Shepherd in the way of His choice. It matters not where the Great Shepherd leads. All will be well. We have the unquestionable promise of His PRESENCE. What more do we need? Paul says, in II Corinthians 3:5: "Our sufficiency is of God."

The shepherd boy never took his flock anywhere he had not already been himself. All the dangers - flooding rivers, rockslides, poisonous plants, blinding storms of sleet, hail or snow – were familiar to David. He had handled his sheep and managed them with care under every weather condition. Nothing took him by surprise. Likewise, in every dark trial and every dismal disappointment or distressing dilemma, the Christian can say, "I will not fear, for Thou are with me."

THE DREADED VALLEY - In our previous studies, we watched the shepherd tenderly care for his sheep, leading them to "green pastures" and then "still waters." Wanderings of the flock were restored as he led them over "right paths" toward home. There were time, though, when it was necessary to go through the dreaded "valley of the shadow of death."

Actually, there is such a valley in Palestine. One writer describing this valley said, "Every sheepherder from Spain to Israel knows of it. It is south of the Jericho road leading from Jerusalem to the Dead Sea, and is narrow to file through a mountain range. Climatic and grazing conditions make it necessary for the sheep to be moved through this valley for seasonal feeding each year.

"This valley is four and a half miles long. The sidewalls are over 1,500 feet in places. It is only ten or twelve feet wide at the bottom. Travel through the valley is dangerous because its floor is badly eroded by cloud-bursts causing gullies 7 or 8 feet deep. Actually, footing on some of the rock is so narrow in so many places that the sheep cannot turn around. It is an unwritten law of shepherds that the flocks must go up the valley in the morning hours, and down in the evening time, lest flocks meet at defile

After halfway through the valley, the walk crosses from one side to another to a place where the path is cut in two by an eight-foot gulley. One section of the path is about 18 inches higher than the other. The sheep must jump across it. The shepherd stands at this break and coaches, or forces his sheep to make the leap. If a sheep slips and lands in the gulley, the shepherd's crook is encircled around the large sheep's neck, or a small sheep's chest, and it is lifted to safety.

Many wild dogs lurk in the shadows of the valley, looking for their prey. After a band of sheep has entered the defile, the leading sheep may come upon such a dog. Unable to react, the leader 'baas' a warning. The shepherd, who's skilled in throwing his rod, hurls it at the dog and knocks the animal into the washed-out gulley, where he is killed. Thus, the sheep have learned to fear no evil in the valley of the shadow of death, for their master is there to aid them and protect them from harm."

What is the valley of the shadow of death about of which David speaks? Though this verse has been quoted by saints in every age for comfort and assurance at death, it would seem from verse 5 that David was not thinking primarily of death, for indeed there are no enemies "in the presence" of the believer after he dies. He used the visible presence of the Lord immediately "to dwell in the house of the Lord forever." He was conscious of the great truth that when the believer closes his eyes in physical death, at that instance, the believer is transported into a glorious presence of the Lord.

I believe that "the valley of the shadow of death" refers to the many trials of life that believers must face. Sorrow and suffering of all kinds are part of the valley experience. It could well refer to the agony often experienced before death or the sorrow that frequently brings down heavily upon loved ones after death, but never death itself. Christ's death and resurrection remove the darkness from death. So, with the true believer in Christ, death is the gate of entry into the presence of our Lord.

ILLUSTRATION: A fire destroyed Thomas Edison's laboratory. Many unfinished experiments were burned beyond recognition. The scientists, while walking through the wreckage, found a little package of papers tied together with a string. The package was water-soaked and fire-scarred, but by some freak of chance, it was left secured. Thomas Edison opened it, and at the center of the wrappings was a photograph of himself that was burned around the edges, but still undamaged. He looked at it for a little while and then he picked up a piece of charcoal from the floor and wrote across the face of the picture: "IT DIDN'T TOUCH ME."

The psalmist says, "I will fear no evil." Why? Because "the Lord is my shepherd." David had inner assurance that knowing God is our shepherd, nothing – not even the shadow of death – can touch us. Until our Great Shepherd calls us to "abide in the house of the Lord forever," we must follow Him even through strange paths that may lead us into sickness or sorrow or suffering. The Bible does not promise freedom from discomfort or anguish in this life. Rather, we see just the opposite. Job writes, "Man is born into trouble." (Job 5:7)

Trials are to be expected. Christians are by no means immune. We must never forget the way of the cross is not a path of ease and comfort. Indeed, the Lord told His disciples, "In the world you shall have tribulation." They were not to despair.

STANDING IN THE SHADOW OF DEATH - As a young boy, David had stood in the shadow of death. His faith was verified as he approached Goliath. David was perhaps the most unlikely person to be used by God. We can imagine what David was really like.

David had the poetic genius of a Shakespeare, the musical ear of a Beethoven, the hand-eye coordination of Andre Agassi, coupled with a military genius that has never been duplicated in history.

APPROACHING GOLIATH – David picked up five smooth stones. Why did he pick up five stones? Someone suggested that it was the custom of the day, like three strikes in baseball, two serves in tennis or four downs in football. The other person mentioned that the extra stones were for Goliath's four brothers. I do not think that David did everything as important as this simple act of preparation just because of tradition, rules or the fashion of the hour.

Why did David choose five stones when only one was needed to defeat the giant? Since I was a child, I remember the story of this small boy called David facing Goliath. What to me and others is a simple toy and a few rocks has fascinated all of us. Even though we must admit that he trusted God in everything as he stood before the giant, this boy had spent all of his life to acquire the skill necessary to effectively use this deadly weapon. This biblical situation is clearly evidence that God was on the side of the army with the heaviest artillery. David's faith coupled with a slingshot and stones.

This shepherd boy that we know as David could probably split a hair with his right or left hand at forty feet. When the rock left the sling, it traveled at the rate of approximately 200 feet per second and delivered a thrust of about 500 pounds. Incidentally, this compares with the power of a Colt 45.

Well, we still haven't answered the question – why five stones? I think that David's computer-like mind was saying, "I've killed the lion and the bear. I do not think a giant's skull is any thicker, but if one stone doesn't stop him, I will have time for four others. The first shot, I will put in the temple. That just slows him down, then I'll shoot one in each ear. I'll have one left for each eye. If he's coming after all these stones, I'm finished."

Why five stones? Those rocks illustrate the humility of David. We have the idea that a champion says, "Oh, I'm not very good." That's false humility. Humility is knowing the following: "I'm a champion, but without the Lord that's all I am."

In the valley of the shadow of death, David used all his resources and abilities. Indeed, the Lord is with us during difficult days and in unusual circumstances, but He expects us to use the gifts and available supplies which are ours.

I WILL MEET NO EVIL - The psalmist did not write "I will meet no evil." He said, "I will FEAR no evil. Evil will come, but I will not fear it for Thou art with me." It is in this high and important relationship with God that the shepherd affirms that he was beyond the reach of trouble. Every tunnel has light at both ends.

a) Fear is a real problem that we face. This emotion goes far back in human history. Nobody completely escapes it. We hear plenty about sin, but the church is almost completely silent concerning fear. This was not true of Jesus. He said, "Go and sin no more," in John 8:11. He also said, "Fear not," and "Be not afraid," and "Be not anxious."

    b) Fear drains strength from us. It depletes our resources. It strangles the spirit from life and imprisons us. It paralyzes life. Often, we use this expression: "He was scared stiff," or "He was scared to death." Our phobias come in numerous varieties. Fear of others, fear of ourselves, fear of change, fear of height, fear of enclosed places, fear of growing old, fear of disease, fear of poverty. Fear is an emotion of extremely high velocity.

ILLUSTRATION: Do you remember this in the Garden of Eden? Adam discovered what people have found to be true throughout the years. As soon as the first man had eaten the forbidden fruit, he said, "I was afraid, and hid myself." (Genesis 3:10) Does that sound familiar? "I was afraid." "I hid." We sin and then what happens? Conscience begins to knock on our door. Guilt enters into our lives and brings us comfort. We sin again, and suddenly we have a habit on our hands. Sin comes dressed in the garments of so-called "freedom."

    c) To be free from fear, a person must live an upright life. If you have this kind of life, do not lose it. If you have lost this kind of life, recover it. Nothing is as effective in taking fear from your life as an awareness deep within of the Shepherd's nearness. "I will fear no evil, for Thou art with me."

    d) Higher Ground. I hear many people wanting to be on "higher ground" with God to climb above the lowlands of life. However, we go to higher ground just as ordinary sheep go. There's only one way there – by climbing UP through the valley and not DOWN through the valleys. Every mountain has its valley. The best way to the top is always through the valley.

ILLUSTRATION: I read some time ago a story that Dr. Richard Hudson tells about his visit to Scotland with a friend. Sometimes, they rode bicycles or traveled on horseback, but most of the time they walked. One day, they came to a picturesque inn on a lake where they spent the night.

The following day, they were talking to the innkeeper concerning a trail they would take as they continued their journey. "You are three or miles from the most beautiful lake in Scotland," the innkeeper said. "Lake Lochy."

"Tell us how to get there," Hudson requested. Soon their new friend had given directions for a long, round-about route.

"Isn't there a closer way?"

"Yes. You can go down through the valley. We call it the 'Dark Mile.' The trail extends through a deep gorge. It is dark, gloomy, the vegetation is pale, the water drips from the frightening overhanging cliffs. No one goes through the Dark Mile unless there is not other alternative."

Nevertheless, Dr. Hudson and his friend took the nearest route. In the middle of that valley, there were tremendous walls of rock on both sides of the tiny path. It was so dark that when they looked up, they could see the stars. They continued to walk through that damp, forbidden place.

Suddenly, they came out over a little ridge that looked out overlooking a magnificent. You guessed it. It was Lake Lochy. Hudson and his companion just gasped in excitement. They would never forget the sight. The friend remarked, "You know, if we had not walked through the dark valley, I don't believe we would ever have appreciated the beauty of Lake Lochy.

Through the Dark Mile, the valley of the shadow, God calls us deeper into life. The word I emphasize is the word *through* in this verse. Sometimes there is no alternative path. Sometimes we must go through the dark mile with the promise of God that we will go <u>through it.</u>

In this verse, the psalmist was referring to the dark valley of DEATH; however, to the Christian, even the valley of death becomes a tunnel with light at both ends. At every memorial service for those who know Christ, down through the years, I've read at least a portion of the 23rd Psalm. I remind those in attendance of the most important word of comfort found in the psalm is the word *through* with the word *shadow*. The psalmist said, "Yea, though I walk through...." This is the victory that Christ gives to those who know Him as Shepherd and Lord.

All of us understand what it means to be in a valley. Those who have gone down into the valley with the Lord know that danger is there. Only by going through the valley can we reach the high country. Thorns may cut us and rip us, enemies may attack us, the rivers may overwhelm us and threaten to drown us, but God is in this situation with us, and we "shall not fear."

I think one of the great miracles of this scripture is that the psalmist did not ask to escape the shadow of death. The psalmist did not even ask so that he might not be afraid. Instead, he affirmed that he would not be afraid and, then he wrote one of the greatest truths of the world. God will be there, too. The presence of God was the secret of the psalmist's fearlessness. Death cannot be evaded, but "I will fear no evil for Thou are with me." Here, David was not writing ABOUT a person; he was talking TO a person. "Thou art with me."

Notice the other word that I mentioned – **shadow.** I think this is the key. He'll walk with us through the valley of the SHADOW of death. You see, a car can hit you and destroy you, but the shadow of a car cannot touch you. A dog can bite you, but the shadow of a dog cannot touch you. Death can come to the believer, but it shall not touch him because Jesus said, "He who believes in Me shall never die." The old house that you and I live in may wear out and decay and will die, but the real you never tastes death, for the Bible says, "To be absent in the body is to be present with the Lord."

ILLUSTRATION: A soldier asked his commanding officer is he could go to no man's land between the trenches to bring back one of his buddies who laid seriously wounded.

"You may go," said the office, "but it is too late. It's not worth the risk. Your friend is probably dead, and you will throw your own life away."

But, the soldier went. Somehow he managed to reach his friend, lift him on his soldier and bring him to safety. The two of them tumbled together and lay in the bottom of the trench.

The officers looked tenderly at the rescue and said, "I told you it wouldn't be worth it. Your friend is dead and you are critically wounded."

"It was worth it, sir."

"How do you mean 'worth it?' I tell you, your friend is dead."

"Yes, sir," the hero answered, "but it was worth it because when I got to him, he said, 'I knew you'd come.'"

The soldier did not save his friend from the shadow experience, but he altered the effect of the experience.

Is Jesus your Lord? Is He your Shepherd? Do you know this because of your personal experience with Him? If He is, then you have already discovered that in every valley, as in every tunnel, there is a light at both ends.

VIII. THE PROTECTION

Verse 4 - *"Thy rod and thy staff they comfort me."*

The trip through the valley of the shadow of death was not very pleasant. All along the way, there was the constant danger of poisonous snakes and vicious animals waiting to devour their prey. But, with careful guidance and leadership, the shepherd cautiously, through the cold, damp valley, prepared for any emergency. How did he prepare?

I. THE SHEPHERD'S ARMOR

The first weapon that the shepherd possessed is known as the "rod." This was his weapon in the event of an attack. The rod was a club about 2 feet long made from a small tree with a root that had been rounded off into a ball about the size of a man's fist. Into this, the shepherd drove a number of spikes about 2 inches long. Usually one blow from the rod would kill or disable any foe. A noose ran through the handle end so the rod could be attached to the belt. When in action, this noose was wrapped around the waist to prevent the rod from being dropped or struck from the shepherd's hand.

Every shepherd boy spent hours practicing with the rod, learning how to throw it with amazing speed and accuracy. This club was the main weapon used for defense of himself and his sheep. It was the symbol of strength, power and authority as a shepherd.

Some years ago, there was a teacher of a first grade class who asked the youngsters to illustrate the 23rd Psalm. After they read the chapter carefully, each child chose a particular phrase and diligently began his work.

Several students molded shepherds with their sheep from homemade clay. Some splashed paint on brown paper and outlines small streams and deep valleys. Those are part of "the house of the Lord." The remainder of the boys and girls chose plain pieces of paper from the apple supply and drew scenes with felt tipped watercolor pens.

At the conclusion of the hour, the teacher let them tell about their masterpieces. Most of the artwork was easily identified. However, one picture puzzled even this long-time worker.

Jimmy's scene depicted a man in a brown suit with a tie, seated behind a huge desk. All around were men and women standing as though they were listening to his every word. He explained, "This is Rod and his staff."

When God called Moses, the desert shepherd, and sent him to deliver Israel from Egypt's bondage, the rod was used to demonstrate Moses' power and authority. It was always through Moses rod that miracles were accomplished to convince Pharaoh of Moses' divine commission and to give confidence to the people of Israel. The rod represents God's mind and will. It implied authority and carried with it the convincing power and the impact of the Old Testament terminology; "Thus saith the Lord."

I want to remind all of us that there is comfort in seeing the rod in the shepherd's hand. In our day, there should be assurance in our hearts as we see the authority of the Word of God, for the scriptures are God's rod, an extension of His mind, will and intentions.

ILLUSTRATION: The Associated Press carried the story of a man who lived in this country illegally for thirty years. The immigration authorities discovered the fact and took steps to deport him. Digging into the case, they found themselves confronted with an unusual international dilemma. The alien stood before officials, waving his arms, and in his broken English tried to tell them that they could not deport him. The small country in Central Europe in which he was born no longer existed because of the shifting boundaries after the war. His country was wiped out.

A similar experience has happened to all of us. The land of our birth, the land of our childhood, is not here anymore. You say, "How is that?" We live in a different world where numerous confusing voices and strange philosophies are presented. Society today has a so-called code of morals that is not moral at all; it is absolutely immoral. If we are to experience the Christian life of joy, we must regularly and systematically turn to the Word of God and discover in its pages the Shepherd's hand of authority. This exacting, powerful instrument is the only weapon that we can use to keep out confusion among chaos. Thus the psalmist wrote: "Thy rod comforts me."

The shepherd used the rod for discipline or warning. If he observed a sheep wandering away, approaching poisonous weeds, or getting too close to danger, the rod would go whistling through the air sending the wayward animal rushing back to the flock.

ILLUSTRATION: Around the turn of the century, a fire chief in San Francisco went to the city council. "Gentlemen," he said, "you have made a serious mistake. The main line of the water supply for this city passes over the Saint Andreas fault." This brilliant man explained that if the city ever had a major earthquake, it would occur at the Saint Andreas fault and that the waterline would be severed. "There will be no way for us to extinguish all the fires which would seep the city." The council heard the plea, and they understood the rationale of the chief, but because of other matters, they tabled this problem to consider at a later date.

Several years passed. In 1906, an earthquake shook San Francisco; the waterline was broken. The uncontrollable fire that ensued snuffed out the lives of nearly seven hundred people. Four-fifths of the city was leveled because water was not available to stop the catastrophe. The fire chief who had issued a warning was killed in the fire as his home collapsed at the first impact of the earthquake.

How many times has God admonished us about the wages of sin? How often in our study of the Scriptures have we been impressed with the fact that the Spirit of God was calling us back to the point of beginning again with Him? The Word of God comes to our hearts with surprising suddenness for correction and reproof when we tend to go astray.

The shepherd's rod was also employed for counting the sheep. In the Old Testament we read of passing under the rod (Lev. 27:32). When a sheep passed under the rod, it had been counted and examined with great care. A sheep externally might look all right, but because of its long wool, some disease could be hidden from the Shepherd.

The second piece of armor the shepherd carried was the staff. The staff he carried was like a scout-pole. It was about six to eight feet in length. It had a multitude of uses. Shepherds often had refreshing naps while leaning on the top of the staff. It is interesting to observe that the word *bridge* does not appear even one time in the Bible. The streams were crossed in rainy season by putting a staff in the middle of the stream and leaping to the other side.

More than any other items, the staff identified the shepherd. In no other profession was the shepherd's staff carried. It was uniquely an instrument used in the care and management of sheep – designed, shaped, and adapted especially for their needs.

The staff also was extended to catch individual sheep, young or old, and draw them close to the shepherd for examination. It was most useful for the shy and timid sheep that usually stayed away from the shepherd. With it, he brought them back into the flock and to himself. The staff was helpful in directing and guiding the flock. It was employed to direct them onto a new path or to push them through a gate or through a long, difficult route. The shepherd would lay the tip of the stick gently against the animal's side, apply pressure, and steer the sheep in the way he wanted it to go.

You say, "What does that really mean to me?" Well, the Holy Spirit performs exactly the same function in our lives.

ILLUSTRATION: E. Stanley Jones was lost once in the jungles of India and secured a native from the area to guide him back to civilization. For many hours the man cut through the bush. Being ignorant of the jungle, Dr. Jones asked, "Where is the path?"

The guide glanced at him and replied, "Sir, I am the path." This is what Jesus affirms, "I am the way. I am the path."

Many times in our journey, we face decisions that are totally confusing. When the Spirit of God has been making us like Jesus, the mind of the Good Shepherd is within us, and He becomes the way.

I remember, after I was saved, that soon after called me to preach at the age of 16. I realize that the Christian was life was in several stages. Stage one – it's easy. Stage two – it's hard. Stage three – it's impossible. Stage four – it's exciting. Stage five – it's very important. I am sharing that with you to tell you that we are to grow in our Christian journey, and we are to be filled with the Holy Spirit who will empower us and enable us to live in victory.

We cannot fulfill the demands of Jesus Christ without a daily infilling. When we sincerely desire His guidance and ask Him to control our lives, He gives us more of life that we ever dreamed possible.

We have a Great Shepherd who protects His sheep from all enemies. You say, "If only I could get the victory over this one thing, I could really count for Christ." You are a possessor of victory; you need only claim it. You'll find, in Romans 6:14, "Sin shall not have dominion over you." Hold on to that truth. Listen to it. Sin shall have dominion over you. I am not talking about sinless perfection; I am speaking of daily, victorious living in the power of Christ.

Major Whittle one time read the hymn *I Need Thee Every Hour*. He dropped the hymnal and said, "That will never do. I need Him every moment." Immediately, he sat down and wrote the words to that inspiring hymn that has meant so much to us:

> "*Moment by moment, I'm kept in His love,*
> *Moment by moment, I have life from above.*
> *Looking to Jesus till glory does shine,*
> *Moment by moment, O Lord, I am thine.*"

Victorious living is a moment-by-moment experience. There is no dedication experience great enough to last a lifetime. We need a daily experience with the Lord if we expect to overcome sin. This is a supernatural walk.

One of my favorite comic strips is "Peanuts." If you have read anything about "Peanuts," you'll see Charlie and Lucy with a football. How funny some of those incidents have been! In one cartoon, Charlie Brown is quite certain that Lucy offered to hold the ball, for his placekick will end up as all the other attempts have. She'll hold the ball, and exactly as he's ready to kick, his foot will go into the air and he will end up flat on his back. He said to her, "You must think I'm crazy. You said you'll hold the ball, but you won't. You'll pull it away like you always have, and I will break my neck."

With a heavenly look, Lucy responded, "Why, Charlie, how you talk....I wouldn't think of such a thing!" I'm a changed person. Look, isn't this a face you can trust?"

Since Charlie Brown is Charlie Brown, he accepts Lucy at her word. "Alright, you hold the ball, and I'm running up to kick it."

Sure enough, the expected happens. He flies through the air, smashes to the ground, and he can only scream, "She did it again! She did it again!"

In the last scene, a proper Lucy leans over to Charlie and chuckles, "I admire you, Charlie Brown. You have such great faith in human nature."

There are a lot of Lucy's in the world. Many people tragically do not trust anybody. They do not trust themselves and they don't think anybody else is trustworthy. Some live by Abraham Lincoln's observation: "You can fool all of the people some of the time, and you can fool some of the people all of the time."

The whole story of mankind is a history of persons not keeping faith with others. Wars have been started, businesses have failed, marriages have been destroyed, families have been shattered, individuals have been proven deficient because one person or another in the relationship did not keep trust alive and well.

Do you remember what is quoted on our coins in America? "In God We Trust." That is exactly what we must do again. We need to trust completely the members of our family and those are within the framework of the church. Officials who have been elected to high office should have our complete support until their corruption and immorality have been proven beyond the shadow of a doubt. We must restore confidence in our society by being Christians who are almost naïve in simplicity compared to the standards of the world. By trusting people who come begging and exploiting, let us pray that they will see in us the possibility of what they can become.

I'm not referring to an ignorant trust. That's not a solution. Anyone who blindly depends on another and who believes in him without being conscious of that person's flaws, imperfections, and limitations will certainly be the victim of tragedy. I am talking about a basic trust in the Good Shepherd, a personal relationship with Jesus Christ, which includes a plan of love, acceptance, and brotherhood – the genius of God's kingdom in this world.

I realize we have evil in our world today. So many people are afraid. Sometimes all of us feel helpless, and we are until we find comfort in realizing that God's hand and power are involved in history. Listen to it again – "Thy rod and thy staff they comfort me." Now, my dear friend, that is good news!

IX. THE PERIL

Verse 5 - *"Thou preparest a table before me in the presence of my enemies."*

As the shepherd led his sheep over a long journey to a good, rich pastureland, he was always confronted by many dangers along the way. There was the dread from above as eagles and vultures would sweep down upon the flock and steal the lambs. All around, there were unseen enemies in hiding. There were beasts of all kinds waiting for their chance to attack. Wolves, jackals and even lions were a constant threat to the Palestinian shepherd and his sheep.

Often, little brown adders living underground came up to nip the nose of the sheep as they grazed, producing death many times. In addition to all of this, thieves and robbers were a constant hurt to the shepherd and his flock.

There were other perils to be encountered, but one of the shepherd's greatest problems was that of poisonous plants. The sky may be free of enemies and perfect harmony all around, but mixed in the beautiful and luscious grass there may be a very dangerous enemy. Poisonous plants, which are fatal to sheep, are found in the Holy Land. The shepherd must "prepare" the pasture.

After much hard work, the shepherd leads the sheep into a "prepared pasture," which is free from perils and the presence of other deadly plant enemies.

As children of God, we always follow the Great Shepherd, our Lord and Master, over the great pathways of life. We are plagued by many enemies, but the Shepherd never loses a sheep. The Lord Jesus says, in John 10:27, 28, "My sheep hear my voice. I know them and they follow me. I have given unto them eternal life, and they shall never perish." If we follow the Shepherd, we are secure from all enemies.

Someone, I'm sure, will ask, "Is this all one needs to do to be sure of eternal life? Do I just simply believe on Jesus Christ to be my personal Savior?" Absolutely! This is all you CAN do, for God says, "By grace are you saved through faith, and not of yourselves. It's the gift of God, not of works, lest any man should boast." (Ephesians 2:89)

A missionary was going from bed to bed in a hospital, speaking with the patients about the Lord Jesus. She came upon an undeveloped, under-sized little boy whose white face caught her eye because of his deep, deep concern. When she first talked to him about the Lord, he seemed to have little interest, but he became more and more concerned. He argued that he attended church, and thought this was sufficient. Powerfully and carefully, the missionary told him of our wonderful Lord Jesus, who alone could serve. She made other calls on this little fellow, but she was unwilling to make a commitment to Jesus. One morning, when the missionary called, she found the boy beaming with a newfound joy.

"What has happened?" she asked. "Oh, I always knew that Jesus was necessary, but I never knew until yesterday that He was enough."

Praise God, He is enough! Wouldn't it be wonderful if everyone could make this discovery?

David had encountered many enemies along life's way, but the Lord always gave deliverance. In fact, one day David wrote, in Psalm 3:7, "Thou has smitten all my enemies." Like sheep, believers in Christ must face many enemies. Consider the eagle and the vultures of the air, ever swooping upon us and trying to snatch our "joy unspeakable" from us. In fact, Paul tells us in Ephesians 6:12 about "spiritual wickedness in high places."

Not only are there enemies above, they are below as well. As sheep might be bitten anytime by a snake underfoot, so you and I need to watch out for that old serpent called the devil and Satan, which deceived the whole world. (Revelation 12:9) "Satan is more subtle than any beast of the field," according the Genesis 3:1. He always looks for an opportunity to instill the poison of doubt into your mind and heart.

Even though Satan and all of his demons are defeated in Christ, and even though Satan is the prince of this world and the god of this age, he is a defeated foe. When Satan tempts us to doubt God, we should answer him from the Word of God like the Lord Jesus did. To each temptation, Jesus responded with a counter statement from the scriptures. Through Christ, we may meet Satan in the same victorious manner.

A story is told of a school boy who came to know the Lord Jesus through that wonderful verse – John 5:24, that says, "Verily, verily I say to unto you – ye that heedeth My word and believeth on Him that hath sent me has everlasting life and shall not come into condemnation, but is passed from death into life." When the boy arrived home and was sitting in the living room, he was tempted to doubt. He felt it was all a mistake. The temptation became so fierce that the boy thought Satan was actually under the chair, talking to him. For awhile, the inexperienced lad did not know how to answer Satan, but then he got an idea. Quickly, he reached for his bible, turned to John 5:24. Pointing his finger to the verse, he reached under the chair and said, "There you are, Satan. Read it for yourself." The boy, in recounting the incident later, said,

"It seemed, in that moment, that the devil disappeared." Satan cannot stand the Word of God.

Not only were the shepherds and his helpless sheep plagued by snakes and vultures, but also were in constant danger of thieves laying in wait, ready to steal the sheep from the shepherd. This suggests to me the ungodly companions ever trying to turn the believer away from the Lord Jesus. I have thought many times how many broken hearts might have been spared had the Christian boy or girl obeyed God's eternal principle. "Be ye not unequally yoked together with unbelievers." (II Corinthians 6:14) Many a testimony has been ruined because careless Christians were not prudent in choosing the kind of friends that pleased the Lord.

The perils that confront the true believer are many, but to my mind, there is one that exceeds them all. We spoke of the poisonous plant intermixed with the good grass. This brings to mind the noxious weed of "self" that engulfs the usefulness of all believers. The Great Shepherd desires to pluck it out of our hearts. We still feed upon its poison. Probably, you and I have no greater enemy.

A minister was asked one time at a minister's conference, "What is the chief problem in your work for God?" His straightforward and honest answer was, "My self." I believe you and I have the same problem.

The Lord longs to fill us with Himself, but He cannot until we are empty of ourselves. It was D.L. Moody who said, "Christ sends none away empty but those who are full of themselves." There has never been a selfish person in the world that has been a great Christian.

What do you think the great secret of Paul's mighty usefulness really is? It can all be summed up in one word -

SELFLESSNESS. He was completely empty of "self." He had no interest in his own personal gain or comfort. He said, in Philippians 3:7, "What things were gained to me, those I counted loss for Christ." He was never insistent on carrying out his own wishes and plans. He could simply say, "For me to live is Christ." (Philippians 1:21)

Neither did Paul boast of himself in is own works. He said, in Galatians 6:14, "God forbid that I should glory save in the cross of the Lord Jesus Christ. His basic interest and desire in life was summed up in Philippians 1:20, "So now also Christ shall be magnified in my body, whether it be by life or by death, that only God would put this earnest desire in our hearts.

I believe if Christ is truly the supreme focus in our lives, our enemies would quickly vanish under the mighty arm of the Great Shepherd. Eat at the table of blessing that He has prepared for us in the midst of our enemies.

X. THE POWER

Verse 5 -*"Thou anointest my head with oil."*

After a long, eventful day, the sheep returned to the fold. As they would enter the door single file, the shepherd quickly examined the sheep for briars in his wool, or scratches or bruises. If any of these sheep were found, they were removed from the line until others had passed. The shepherd then would give his attention to the needy sheep. Each would was carefully cleansed and then the shepherd dipped his hand into an earthen bowl of olive oil, and anointed the wound. Thus, the sheep remained comfortable and ready for a night of refreshing rest.

David said of the Lord, "Thou anointest my head with oil." Doubtless, he was thinking of the many times Jehovah had ministered to him when he was tired in body and distressed in soul. But, there's probably a deeper meaning. Oil, in the scriptures, often symbolized the Holy Spirit. Without the Spirit's power, the believer service to God is useless. In fact, David had found this to be true even though sad in his own life. There were times in David's life that he sensed his own lack of power. In Psalm 6:2, he prayed, "Have mercy on me, O Lord, for I am weak. O Lord, heal me for my bones are vexed." In the midst of his own weakness and frailty, David found God's mighty power to be sufficient. Listen to what he says in Psalm 59:16, "I will sing of Thy power, yea, I will sing aloud of Thy mercy." Then, in Psalm 62:11, he further says, "Power belongeth unto God."

It's the same truth we need today to realize so greatly in our lives, as well as our church's life. Listen to that statement again: "Power belongeth unto God." Our churches are well-organized, well-planned – and we have very interesting and challenging programs. Our music today is the finest. Sermons are eloquent and scholarly, but why are lost souls not repenting and crying out to the Living God for salvation?

Even though figures show today that church membership is at an all-time high, joining a church is considered to be on the same plane as joining a lodge or club. There is no noticeable between the world and the church. In fact, some of our church people do the same thing the unchurched people do. There appears to be little transformation of life and character. Consequently, the church is devoid of the Holy Spirit's power to win the lost to Christ.

In our day, however, it is quite popular for one to make a profession of faith in Christ and join the church. It gives position and prestige. It may even help one's business by opening the way for new contacts. Is this what God intended for His church? If we are to make an imprint and an impact in a world of sin with the Gospel of Christ, like the shepherd's over-flowing cup of oil, our lives must flow with the fullness of the Holy Spirit.

We must never forget that our Lord performed all His mighty works in the strength and energy of the Holy Spirit. Do you remember how his ministry began? With the anointing of the Spirit. In Luke 4:18, we have the words of our Savior concerning Himself, which were read in the synagogue at Nazareth on the Sabbath Day. This was a prophecy given by Isaiah many years before: "The Spirit of the Lord is upon me because He anointed me to preach the Gospel to the poor." There's one thing obvious from that verse just quoted…the Lord Jesus was definitely anointed and empowered by the Holy Spirit to carry on His ministry. In fact, He considered the Holy Spirit's work so sacred and important that, when he was accused by the Pharisees of healing in the power of the devil, he declared such action to be unpardonable. He said, in Matthew 12:31-32, "Wherefore, I say unto you all manner of sin and blaspheming shall be forgiven unto men, but the blaspheming of the Holy Ghost shall not be forgiven unto men." If the Lord Jesus gave such emphasis to the important recognition of the Holy Spirit, certainly we who are His followers should give this same respect in our hearts.

Without the fullness of God's power through the Spirit, believers accomplish little for the Lord. It is for this reason that God commands us "to be filled with the Spirit." (Ephesians 5:18) We don't have to beg or plead for the fullness of the Spirit, but simply meet the requirements and the Spirit's fullness and power will be known. You ask me, "What are the requirements?" There are just two: a) remove every obstacle and hindrance from the life, and b) receive the glorious promise by faith.

Dr. James H. McCartney used to explain it to us while standing on the wall of a great dock. Outside was a huge lake vessel about to enter. At his feet lay the empty lock waiting...but for what? Waiting to be filled. Beyond lay the great Lake Superior with its limitless abundance of supply. It, too, was waiting. Waiting for what? Waiting for something to be done at the lock, e'er the great lake could pour in its fullness. In a moment, it was done. The lockkeeper reached out his hand, touched a steel lever, and a little, wicked gate sprang open under the magic touch. At once, the water began to boil as it seethed. Dr. McCartney saw it rapidly creeping up the walls of the rock. In a few moments, the lock was full. The great gates swung open, the huge ship floated into the lock now filled to the brim with fullness.

What is this but a picture of the great truth of the fullness of the Holy Spirit? Here are God's children like that empty lock, waiting to be filled. As that great, inland sea outside the lock was waiting and willing to pour its abundance into the lock, so God is willing to pour His fullness into the lives of all His children. He is waiting, but you say, "For what?" Waiting as the lake waited for something to be done by us. Waiting for us to reach forth and touch the lever of complete dedication to His will. Let's open the gates of our hearts through which abundant life and power shall flow and fill. God is ready and willing. Why wait? All the barriers and hindrances are on our side. We have the privilege of opening the door to His power. Christians, let us remove the obstacles. It may cost us our selfishness, our pride, our inconsistency or many other things, but whatever it is, it is well worth it. Let's let them go. Open the door and receive God's fullness.

Greatest of all is the power for service. Jesus said, in Acts 1:8, "You shall receive power. After that, the Holy Ghost is come upon you and ye shall be witnesses unto me." We must never forget this thought: we are not filled merely to be happy, but to be useful. God never wastes or squanders His power. The spirit-filled man will always be busy for God, seeking to lead people to Christ.

Our greatest need, I think, in the twenty-first century is for us and our churches to sense the need of this power. Now, some do, but many do not. We do have all the machinery, but we need the power. Here is a great newspaper press capable of turning out thousands of papers an hour. It is ready to begin its operation, but it lies silent and helpless, incapable of printing even one paper. "What's wrong?" you ask. Throw the switch, and immediately contact is made. Thus, the power is released and rushes in; the great press is alive and in movement with great power.

In our day, we number more church members than any of the previous age. Our churches are better off financially than ever before. We are given new and improved media with which to effectively proclaim the Gospel. Even with all of this, results are really weak and very few. What's wrong? We must throw the switch. God's power is stored up and ready to flow. Those of us who know the Lord must humble ourselves in His sight and cast out every obstacle to be filled to overflowing for mighty usefulness. What a potential we have in God's power.

We must not ignore this power or fail to use it. God can pack an oak tree into an acorn. He can pack explosive power into an atom, but His greatest power is in the Gospel. He can take a worthless derelict like Jerry McCaughlin of the old Walter Street Mission and transform him into a mighty evangelist for the Lord. Never forget this, my friend – the Gospel is still the "power of God unto salvation." (Romans 1:16)

Christians should be the happiest people in the world. You say, "Why?" Because of God's gracious provision of the overflowing cup of blessing. We sing that old hymn: "There should be showers of blessings..." Indeed, there are showers of blessings falling upon God's people constantly. How we ought to be praising Him for His wonderful love and care. David said it so well in Psalm 107:8: "Oh that men should praise Him for His goodness and for His wonderful works to the children of men." Is it not true, however, that most of us grumble and complain more than we praise?

Let me illustrate how this is so true down through the ages. You might recall, from the first few books of the Bible how God provided the overflowing cup of blessings for the children of Israel. Now, what did they do? They murmured and complained because of the danger and the lack of water and food. Nothing seemed to suit them. They became so disgruntled with everything and everybody that they seldom did anything else but give voice to their grievances. God was not happy about this; in fact, we read in Numbers 11:1, "But the people complained and it displeased the Lord." When believers complain, it always displeases the Lord. Not only does it disturb all those around us, it is a flat denial of God's provision from this overflowing cup of blessings.

The Lord Jesus came into the world that "those who believe on Him might have life, and they might have it more abundantly." (John 10:10) J.P. Phillips translates these words of our Lord's like this: "I came to bring them life, far more life than before." New life in Christ should be a different kind of life. Indeed, it is "far more life than before." Complaining and groaning is of the old life. Believers possess new life in Christ. There is nothing more pathetic than seeing weak Christians trying to preach the living truth to dead sinners. Nothing could be more sickening. How different was John Wesley's witness for Christ? Someone asked him how he got some crowds. "I get on fire for God, and then people come to see me burn!" he replied. Would to God that all across the world Christians were fiery hot for God, filled with His Holy Spirit power!

If we are believers in Christ, and we have been anointed with the Holy Spirit, then we can say with David, "Thou anointest my head with oil." But, are you filled with the Spirit? You should have fruitfulness and usefulness for Christ. If not, surrender all to Him now.

XI. THE PROVISION

Verse 6 - "My cup runneth over."

Having completed the task at dusk of caring for the wounds of his sheep by cleansing them and anointing them with oil, the shepherd now provides for their thirst. In addition to the earthen bowl of olive oil, every sheep fold has a large, cool, stone jar of water with which the shepherd quenches the thirst of his sheep. In drawing his cup out of the jar, the shepherd never has it half or two-thirds filled, but always overflowing and dripping. The sheep eagerly sinks its nose into the refreshing cup and drinks to his satisfaction.

In his days as a shepherd, David held the overflowing cup to his sheep many times. Now he declares of himself, "My cup runneth over." His overflowing was one that never ran dry. It was the cup of the Lord's daily blessings. All who have believed in Christ have the privilege of drinking from this cup. Those outside of Christ can drink only from the cup of wrath. In fact, God tells us in Revelation 16:19 that they must drink "the cup of the wine of the fierceness of Israel."

The wonderful truth is that God's blessings are always overflowing. He not only promises "to pardon us from our sins," but the Bible declares that "He will abundantly pardon." (Isaiah 55:7) Not only is He able to that which we pray, but He is able to do exceedingly, abundantly above all that we ask or think. (Ephesians 3:20) Not only do we have "joy" but "joy unspeakable and full of glory." (I Peter 1:8) In Jesus, we possess not only "peace" but the "peace of God which passes all understanding." (Philippians 4:7) Hallelujah, God has blessed us with all spiritual blessings in heavenly places in Christ, according to Ephesians 1:3.

David also emphasized this in the quote "my cup overflows." He knows that even when there are enemies in sight and the valleys are full of shadows, his cup is full and overflowing, the liquid lapping over the brim. That means, "I have more than enough." God knows how to overflow our situation right where we are.

Do you remember Jesus fed the multitudes by multiplying a tiny amount of loaves and fishes. On each occasion, there were several baskets of leftovers. The Lord had provided those thousands of people with more than enough. Their cup ran over. It also like when Jesus told Peter to go out into the deep and cast his nets. After he fished all night and caught nothing, Peter obeyed, and their catch that morning was enough to rip their nets and almost cause their boat to sink. That's overflowing! God knows how TO SUPERSIZE his provision for every situation. HE gives more than enough.

Sometimes, He will SUPERSIZE a provision of joy for you when there are no great difficulties in your situation. But, He especially SUPERSIZES a provision in the middle of a conflict, a challenge, a hardship or a pain. That's when you know He is real because you know that in such unwelcome circumstances, there is no natural explanation for why you are feeling like this, or why you are not experience joy and fullness.

The Bible says that God has surplus grace. In II Corinthians 9:8, it says, "And God is able to make all grace abound toward you that you always have all sufficiency in all things, and you may have abundance for every good work." For every situation, for all times, in everything God has abundance of grace for us.

He also has a surplus of hope for us. He is the "God of hope," who saturates us with joy and peace so that we may overflow with hope by the power of the Holy Spirit, according to Romans 15:13. "He gives us surplus of joy. He causes you to "rejoice with joy inexpressible and full of glory." (I Peter 1:8) He also provides a surplus of peace. He gives "the peace of God."

Whenever God allows you to get trapped in an inconvenient situation - such as losing a job – it is only to help move you up to the next level of trust in this provision. He wants you to experience His surplus goodness as you look to Him as your major provider.

There are only two times in our lives when God won't meet our physical needs. The first one is when He is trying to strip us of our self-sufficiency. When we are still too independent, He withholds His provision as He works to break us.

The second time is when it is our time to go home. When that moment comes, He won't heal or sustain our body because it is time to leave that body to instead enter His presence.

Apart from these two occasions, we'll always be able to affirm what David testified: "I have never seen the righteous forsaken or the children begging bread." (Psalm 37:25) God is more than faithful to meet our every, physical need.

The story of Dr. H.C. Morrison, as he was returning to this country following a lifetime of missionary service in China, is a very moving story. It so happened that he was coming to the United States on the same ship that carried Teddy Roosevelt. The President had been on a game hunt in Africa. As the ship passed Sandy Hook and came toward the New York harbor, there were signs of welcome all around. Barges floated out with bands and flags. Banners and streamers were everywhere in sight. Five fighting boats sprayed their welcome to the sky.

Morrison realized that all this fanfare was for the President returning from his holiday. Morrison then fell into the grip of self-pity. He knew that no one would be meeting him at the dock. Then, he recalled what he had tried to do in China and how little anyone cared. As he folded his hands and leaned on the deck rail feeling sorry for himself, Mr. Morrison said he heard a voice come to him like a sound of many waters, saying, "But, you are not home yet." I thought of this verse: "They have their reward." (Matthew 6:2) In this life, we may not see all the crooked ways being made straight, but this life is only a glimpse and not a beginning of the pilgrimage for those who really know the Good Shepherd. It is easy to develop the habit of being negative when our attention is fixed on the things of the earth. A boy found a brand new dime and resolved to watch the ground wherever he went for the rest of his life, hoping to find a few more coins. As a result, he acquired a permanent stoop, weak lungs, nearsightedness, no friends and $29.89.

When we always look down, we miss the grandeur and the beauty of the mountains and the stars. God seemed to indicate that there would be sheep in every flock that spend all of their time looking down. While some sheep spend their time looking up at the shepherd, those who look to Jesus are discovering an overflow life.

Are you living in His tableland?

XII. PERMANENCY

Verse 6 – "Surely goodness and mercy shall follow me all the days of my life...."

As we look back on this 23rd Psalm thus far, David has led us step by step as the shepherd of his sheep. But nightfall hastens on and the psalmist sees the sheep safely to the fold.
He recalls how many a night after waiting for all the sheep to rest, that he prepared to settle for his night rest. Laying his rod nearby, just in case of needed protection he wrapped himself in a heavy woolen robe and slept at the entrance to the fold. This whole picture is one of security. It is very probable that with this in mind, David declared, "Surely goodness and mercy shall follow me all the days of my life.

There were times when the sheep returned to the fold at the close of the day, and the shepherd would discover that one of the lambs was missing. As he counted them to find out which one it might be, he also called out and listened as he passed other shepherds, inquiring about the missing sheep. Occasionally it was necessary to go only a short way, but then again he might find it necessary to retrace most of his day's journey. You can imagine how happy the shepherd was when he finally heard some sounds from his lost sheep. Finding him, he lifted him gently, laid him across his shoulders, and headed for home. Along the way, he would shout to the other shepherds whom he had inquired about his sheep to, and would say, "Rejoice with me for I have found my sheep!" What joy he had in his heart to know the lost was found.

Not only is the shepherd's goodness and mercy displayed at night as he seeks a straying sheep, but he carefully watches over them during the daytime as well. As they travelled, the flock was protected both front and back. The shepherd usually had two dogs to provide watchful care from behind. Often when a stray sheep was hurt, the trained dogs barked, attracting the shepherd's attention. The two dogs, "Goodness and Mercy" were always alert to care for the sheep.

Those of us who belong to the GREAT SHEPHERD can say like David with confidence, "Surely Goodness and Mercy shall follow me all the days of my life." Sometimes like sheep, we are disturbed by strange and unfamiliar noises. Some of us have a hard time resting. Need we fear? "He the Keeper will never slumber. The Lord shall preserve thee from all evil. He shall preserve thy soul. He shall preserve they outgoing and thy coming in from this time forward, indeed forever more. (Psalm 121: 3, 7-8)

Sometimes we are prone to worry. We get our eyes on surroundings and off of the Lord. Notice what David does **not** say – "Goodness and mercy shall maybe follow me all the days of my life." He says **"SURELY."** There's not the slightest doubt in his mind. Now some of you are asking as I have asked myself, "Where did David get his marvelous assurance?" Through experience he put God to the test. This is why the Word of God was so real in David's life. You might remember him saying, in Psalm 139:17, "How precious also are the false unto me, O God. How great is the sum of them". He searched the word for the promises of the Lord, and claimed them by faith.

You could not convince David that a life of faith will not work. He knows differently. He had a living faith based upon the knowledge of scriptures, providing perfect peace for the future. In verses 1-5 of the 23rd psalm, David sums up the course of life experiences. When he comes to verse 6 looking back over the past, considering God's faithfulness, he seemed to say, "Surely goodness and mercy will take care of the future as well."

There are times in our lives as Christians when we fail to live a life of commitment and obedience to God. We are like the sheep – we stray from the paths that we have been traveling. We forget all that the Lord has done for us. But praise God, His love does not rest upon our feeble faith. Paul says in I Thessalonians 5:24: "Faithful is He that calleth you, who also will do it." Our GREAT SHEPHERD will not stop loving us. Though my heart may become cold and indifferent, He will always be the same. It reminds me of some words in an old hymn:

O love that will not let me go, I rest my weary soul in Thee.

Can a mother stop loving her son? Of course not – nor can God stop loving His own. Regardless of how wayward a child can be, rarely is there anything that can put out the love in a mother's heart.

The story is told about a mother and her worthless son who were standing before a Christian judge awaiting the boy's sentencing. Many times before the judge had tried to help the youth, but it was all in vain. Finally he said, "I can do no more for this boy. I have done everything I can do. I give up, and advise you – his mother – to do the same."

The mother could not speak at first, but wiping the tears from her eyes, she said, "Judge, I do not blame you. You have been more than kind, and you have gone out of your way to help us. I don't blame you for giving up, but I cannot give up on this boy. I gave him life. I took care of him. I cannot go back on him. <u>He is mine.</u>"

You can be sure that God will do no less than a mother would do for her son. God's perfect love far exceeds the love of parents for their children. David said, in Psalm 27:10,

"When my father and my mother forsake me, then the Lord will take me up."

When we wander from God, He will put "goodness" and "mercy" on our trail. It may even seem that goodness and mercy" have disappeared. They are often in disguise, but they are there. God will never forsake His own. You need only turn around and you will find Him and His "goodness and mercy." Psalm 136:1 says: "The goodness of God endureth forever." If you have wandered away from the Lord, let me urge you to come back to Him. His goodness and mercy will forgive you.

God's goodness and mercy are not temporary gifts. I am assured from the 23rd Psalm that they are my possessions until I meet Christ face to face. These benefits are not for some days but "for all the days of my life." Nor does it mean only the sunny days, but dark as well. Remember this - whatever crosses our paths, whether it be sickness or death or unemployment or a broken heart, "goodness and mercy" are there.

As two shepherd dogs are always near to help and protect, so God has placed goodness and mercy as divine watchdogs to preserve His sheep from all evil. Often times, there appears to a person angels which God declares to be "ministering spirits sent forth to minister for them who shall be heirs of salvation." (Hebrews 1:14) Because of the presence of these divine messengers, we are never alone.

Our Lord knows about loneliness. He went to Gethsemane alone. He went to the cross, alone. He knows what it is to be truly forsaken. If you love Him, you are not alone. He is there. His goodness and mercy are there "all the days of your life."

He "goes before you" to prepare the way. John 10:4 says, "When he putteth forth his sheep, He goeth before them." Psalm 34 says, "The angel of the Lord encamped round about them that fear Him and delivered them." He is "with" you and "in" you providing a constant supply of peace and comfort.

What do we have to fear if we are a child of God? Why should we even worry? God is everlasting in His concern about all of His children. Each person is precious in His sight. This is expressed so vividly in the 23rd Psalm. Have you noticed the personal nature of the psalm? It abounds in personal pronouns. Someone has called it the "pronoun psalm." The first person is referred to many times, as well as the third person. How wonderful that as the believer reads each promise he may say, "Praise God, this is for me!"

Why do we need more from someone who is interested in his own personal problems? Wherever I go, I find that both young and old have problems. Many of them are very serious and very distressing. David had problems also, but he knew what to do with them. He rolled them over to the Lord. To you and me He pleads with confidence. "Cast thy burden upon the Lord and He shall sustain thee. He shall never suffer the righteous to be moved." (Psalm 55:2).

ALL THINGS ARE POSSIBLE TO THEE
OH LORD WE KNOW IT'S TRUE
THE LITTLE THINGS WE CANNOT SEE
THE THINGS WE CANNOT DO

OH PRAISE YOUR NAME SO EASILY DONE,
WITH LITTLE PAIN OR FRET.
YOU HELP US GAIN THE BATTLES WON,
YOU HAVE NOT FAILED US YET.

IT'S WE WHO FAIL TO DO OUR BEST,
IT'S WE WHO FAIL TO MEET THE TEST.

WE LOOK AT THINGS AND GROAN AND SAY,
"I CANNOT GO THROUGHT, I'LL FALL."
BUT OH, YOU HELP US TO OBEY,
HELP US TO CONQUER ALL.

YOU GIVE US STRENGTH IN TIME OF NEED,
ENCOURAGEMENT IN GRIEF.
AND SOMETIMES YOU FROM HEAVEN FEED,
OUR HUNGRY SOULS AND BRING RELIEF.

IT'S WE WHO TAKE YOUR HAND FROM THINE,
WE CANNOT BLAME YOUR NAME DIVINE.

YOU TAKE US OVER ROCKY ROADS,
YOU PULL US FROM THE MIRE.
OH, YOU TAKE AWAY THE LOAD,
AND HELP US TO GO ERE.

THANK YOU FOR EACH TASK, EACH TEAR,
FOR THINGS THAT WEREN'T SO NICE TO DO
BECAUSE AT TIMES IT SEEMED SO QUEER,
OR JUST THE TIMES YOU TOOK US THROUGH.

WE THANK YOU LORD FOR VICTORIES WON,
BUT OH WE KNOW YOU'VE JUST BEGUN.

XIII.   THE PROSPECT

Verse 6 – "*...and I will dwell in the house of the Lord forever.*"

David closes the "prince of psalms" with a clear-cut statement about his prospect for the future. With exception of verse 1, he has been telling of God's immediate and present care. In concluding, he assures us that all of this security that he has enjoyed thus far will continue for eternity. Notice the words "I will dwell in the house of the Lord forever."

So many times this statement refers to the believer's heavenly home. Indeed it does look forward to our future state of blessedness in the presence of the Lord. It is also intended to be a present experience. Heaven begins the moment we are born into the family of God by faith in Christ. It is when we live in fellowship with him that we enjoy the wonderful foretaste of the future glory that will be ours in heaven.

Notice something that I think is very important. David does not say, "Surely goodness and mercy shall follow me all the days of my life" and then "I will dwell in the house of the Lord forever." As" the goodness and mercy" of the Lord followed him, he was already "dwelling in the house of the Lord." In Psalm 27:4, the psalmist writes, "One thing have I desired of the Lord that will I seek after that I may dwell in the house of the Lord all the days of my life to behold the beauty of the Lord and to inquire in His temple." In this passage, he states the paramount desire of his heart. It is not merely a <u>prospect</u> of the future, but it is a <u>possession</u> for the present. David's desire was to live in the presence of the Lord continually. This should be our earnest longing. We are to live not only with a prospect of heaven, but in His present reality. The believer's most consuming passion should be to

109

live in joyful, unbroken fellowship with the Father and His Son through the leadership and guidance of the Holy Spirit.

The question is how may the child of God really know all of these blessings. There is only one way – let the Lord Jesus have absolute and complete control of their entire life. If He is to lead and direct our lives there must be a will and desire on our part to permit him to have the right of way in our hearts. This is so important and it is not easy, but if we are ready, God will do the rest. We will find victory and blessings as we "dwell in the house of the Lord" – now with even a greater prospect for the future.

In the city of Dallas a few years ago, a new highway was under construction. Vast areas were being cleared through the residential sections. Scores of homes had been demolished. Business people driving to and from work were inconvenienced by detours and traffic jams. Familiar landmarks had disappeared. This area would never be the same. The whole project was destructive, disturbing, and expensive. Were this all to be realized from this tremendous sacrifice, it would be extremely hopeless. But thank God, the finished product – the new highway – is now considered a convenience for untold thousands and will be for years to come. It is burdensome now, but highways cannot be constructed in any other way.

It's not easy to give God the right of way to our hearts, but when we do it is so wonderful. It's thrilling. In fact, there is nothing more enjoyable than walking in fellowship with the Lord.

One time, a happy Christian explained to a brother in faith, "It's a GLAD thing to be saved; it's a GRAND thing to be saved."

"Indeed it is," replied the friend, "but I know something better than that."

"Better than being saved?" asked the puzzled Christian. "What can possibly be better than that?"

"The fellowship with the One Who saved me," was the reply.

Those who live in the "house of the Lord" are those who experience the joy of the Lord. In Psalm 16:11, David speaks of the "fullness of joy" known only to believers who are walking with God. "Thou will show me the path of life. In Thy presence there is fullness of joy. At Thy right hand there are pleasures forevermore."

Many, many Christians never know the fullness of joy because of an un-surrendered heart and will. In Ephesians 3:19, Paul prays that the saints at Ephesus might be filled with the fullness of God." Paul knew that if we have the "fullness of God" then we have the "fullness of joy." The only thing that prevents us in this life from knowing blessedness at this very moment is the failure to surrender everything to Christ.

Suppose two young people are planning to be married. Several weeks before the wedding day the young man informs the young bride-to-be that he has a surprise for her. They take a short drive together, and stop in front of a lovely new home. He turns and says, "Here is our new house. I had it built just for us." She is speechless as she gazes in wonder at this marvelous surprise. Moments later they enter and look at each room together. After seeing all the rooms and closets, the young lady recalled that there was one closed door. She asks about it.

"Oh?" says her lover. "You must never go in there. The entire house is yours with the exception of one room. You'll never be allowed in there."

How do you think she must have felt? Her joyfulness would have been clouded very quickly. Unless a change was to occur, I doubt she would even go through with the marriage.

It is doubtful that one contemplating marriage would do such a thing, but do not many Christians treat God in this manner? They reserve one room of the heart for self and sin. They say, "Lord, you can have everything with the exception of this one little room." Until the door of that secret chamber is opened and God is given possession of the heart, it is impossible to know blessings and victory in the heart.

Christian, do you know of anything in your life displeasing to God? Claim the victory immediately! Ask the Lord to clean out every corner of your heart so that you will know the fullness of God's blessings.

It is wonderful to "dwell in the house of the Lord" now, but oh the greater joy will be ours when we dwell there "forever" in the presence of Christ. When David said "forever" he must have been thinking of his shepherding days. To have a home "forever" was a coveted possession for a shepherd. Most of them lived in tents. This kind of life demanded that as soon as the sheep consumed the pasture in any section, the tents had to be moved to a fresh pasture. David rejoiced to know that soon he would be in his eternal home forever in the presence of the Lord.

Listen carefully, for every child of God can hear what God says in II Corinthians 5:1: "For we know that if our earthly house or this tabernacle were dissolved, we have a building with God, not made with hands, eternal in the heavens."

The Lord Jesus expresses a similar truth in John 14:2, when He said, "In my Father's house there are many mansions, abiding places. If it were not so I would have told you. I go to prepare a place for you."

Adequate space for large families was always a problem for families in eastern homes, but in the "place" that our Lord went to prepare, there is plenty of room for those who will enter. It is so good to know that God has prepared a place and that after this life has ended, those who know Him will go to be with Him. What a day of rejoicing and blessing it will be when we come into the full meeting of David's words, "I will dwell in the house of the Lord forever."

As we draw to the close of these teachings on the 23rd Psalm, let us look again to the key that unlocks the door and all the promises presented in the Psalms. "The Lord is my Shepherd." There is no other way to "dwell in the house of the Lord forever" other than the way God has prescribed and allow the Lord Jesus to be our shepherd.

The 23rd Psalm is meaningless until Christ is received as Lord. You may have some knowledge of the psalm and the Shepherd's customs, but it is most important to know the Shepherd personally, and able to say THE LORD IS <u>MY</u> SHEPHERD.

Years ago at a house party, there were many guests present. There was an actor and a saintly old minister. It was requested of the actor to give a recitation. He consented and asked what the guests would like. The 23rd Psalm was suggested. With perfect diction and a clear resonant voice, he recited the psalm much to the admiration of his hearers. They applauded loudly, and then someone suggested that the minister recite the psalm. First, he refused, but upon being urged he closed the Bible and in a voice with deep feeling he slowly repeated familiar verses. The guests soon realized that he was not reciting something merely memorized. He was telling of his own experience with the Shepherd he loved.

There was no applause after he finished. A solemn hush fell upon the audience. After a few moments of silence the actor went to the minister, took his hand and said, "Sir, I know only the psalm, but YOU know the Shepherd."

How about you, dear friend? Do you know the psalm but not the Shepherd? If you do not know the Lord Jesus, invite Him into your life. The 23rd Psalm will immediately become more than beautiful-sounding phrases. It will be a source of refreshing and endless hope in Him who is our Great Shepherd.

TESTIMONY from Michael Justice

About six years after I'd received the Lord Jesus Christ as my Savior, I prayed a collegiate prayer. "Father! Do something in my life to help me trust you more!" Unfortunately, I promptly forgot about it but I truly meant it. I finished college, and started teaching music in south Florida. My plan was to continue in my educational endeavors in that field. To me, life couldn't be better.

Soon, I married a lady named Terri, and marriage was wonderful, but two years later, a crushing blow landed from which we could not escape. Having been previously diagnosed with diabetes, I knew well the dangers and challenges. I began to experience some blurred vision due to hemorrhaging in my eyes. An ophthalmologist diagnosed me as having diabetic retinopathy and suggested an immediate laser treatment. Weeks later, I went totally blind in that right eye. My doctor suggested the laser for my left eye but I refused. Blurry vision was better than none at all.

The early days of visual impairment were scary to say the least. We prayed often in tears, begging God to heal me. Though we expressed great faith in God's power and might, it simply wasn't His plan. While asking God why, the Holy Spirit brought to my memory that old collegiate prayer. I foolishly thought that prayer was a mistake, but faith in God was something He took quite seriously. Retinopathy, a failed laser treatment, and blindness in both eyes was His will to build my faith.

Feelings of anger, sadness, fear, and depression ruled. Some days I could hardly keep back the anger as I taught my classes. But in that grief, I finally made a pact with the Almighty. If He healed me then fine but if not, He would have to be my eyes for the rest of my life.

Years later, He provided the resources for me to go to seminary. My wife was the greatest resource, and without her stubborn faith, who knows what would have happened. I completed one Master's degree then started another to study Greek and Hebrew. .

In my last semester of Hebrew, however, I suffered kidney failure. I started dialysis and the treatments were rough but God carried us through. I was eventually approved for a kidney transplant and told that it would be a two-year wait. Some eight days later, however, the hospital called to tell us that there was a kidney available. Later that night, the surgeon told my wife that the organ started working immediately. I soon went home with a successful transplant, started a new job, and received my second degree.

One week later, however, the doctors discovered that I had contracted Hepatitis C from my donor. The only treatment was a medication that would boost my immune system to fight off the virus. But that also meant that it would start an organ rejection. We had no choice but to sacrifice the transplant or else lose the liver. It was possible that I would need a double transplant.

Kidney rejection raged yet within a week, the lab reports showed no signs of the virus. Just shy of a dialysis chair, **God performed a miracle**! The rejection stopped, and the doctors were amazed. They predicted one year of kidney function, but God gave us seven. When it failed, my gracious wife donated one of hers that is still working well today. Truly, the Lord is my Shepherd and He alone carried me through the valleys of my life.

Michael Justice, Member
Orchard Hills Baptist Church, Garland, Texas

TESTIMONY from Steve Webb

We've been through valleys before. A little over twenty years ago, our son, Tyler died eight hours after he was born. He was born with a herniated diaphragm that caused his lungs to not develop. You never get the answer to the obvious question of "Why, God, did you let this happen?" We got through that time and have since come to realize that God has used our experience to help us help others in similar circumstances.

A few years after that, I had a two-year battle with depression that almost killed me. God used my strong family ties to give me enough hope to "go on" even when I felt God had abandoned me. As a Christian, I know God never abandons us, but the depression tricks your mind into believing that. Little by little, with God's help and some caring friends and family, I was able to regain the emotional control the depression had taken from me. It's still something that I have to guard against even today, all these years later, or depression will sneak up on me and take me down to that pit again.

Then came August 12, 2009. One day earlier my wife had been told she needed major surgery to remove a large fibroid. This news was devastating enough by itself but the next day sent us reeling. Early that Wednesday morning, my doctor's office called with the results from some tests taken on Monday. They were concerned because my white blood cell count was extremely high, so they referred me to another doctor to interpret the results further. Less than two hours later, after phone calls from two different doctors, the nurse on the other end of the line was telling me they were 95% sure I had leukemia. An appointment was set for later that day and I had to call my wife and tell her. I didn't know how to react.

We had watched Pam's grandfather slowly die from leukemia several years ago and that's all I knew of this disease that they had just told me I had. How could I have cancer? At that first appointment, there was more blood testing and the first bone marrow biopsy of several to come. Then the doctor gave us the news that I think devastated me the most. He said they would admit me to the hospital that night and I would be there for up to six weeks, which sounded like an eternity to me. My treatment started the next day and was aggressive and heavy. That first stay was 3½ weeks of pure hell physically, but God taught me more in that 3½ weeks than I had learned in years.

The first thing I realized was that we had dozens of people in our congregation who had either dealt with cancer before or were dealing with it now and I, as their Worship Pastor, had patronized them with a quick "we'll be praying for you" and then gone on with my life as if nothing had ever happened. And it hadn't, until now.

In that first 3½ weeks, I am firmly convinced God healed me. There was a specific time when I felt God's healing hand touch my body and I felt the disease flow from me. That didn't mean that treatment stopped though. The doctors still have to follow their protocol even if they believed I was healed. Through all of the treatments, many hospital stays, and sickness from chemotherapy, God has brought a love between my wife and me that I did not know was possible. He taught me to trust Him with EVERY part of my life - physical, emotional, financial…ALL of it.

My youngest son, Caleb, made me a poster on canvas during that first stay that I can't get away from and I hope I never do. It says simply, "It's hard to stumble when you're on your knees". Because of that poster in my hospital room, I passed my time, praying for everyone I knew who were sick or struggling. I'm firmly convinced that because of the prayers of so many people, many of whom I've never met, God healed me. It's now my turn to return the favor. God spared me for a reason and that reason is not to live for my own self but to live for Him and to lift up those around me. May what I have been through be a testimony of God's grace and my victory in the valley.

Steve Webb, Minister of Music
Orchard Hills Baptist Church, Garland, Texas

ABOUT THE BOOK'S COVER

AUSTIN MANN, expert photographer

It is with heartfelt thanks I acknowledge with gratitude this wonderful photographer who has graciously provided this beautiful image of a valley and volcano's edge in the country of Guatemala for this book's cover.

Only 25 years old, **Austin Mann** is an incredibly talented young photographer who has worked for National Geographic Adventure, McCann-Erickson NYC, Doug Rosa at Rosa+Rosa Inc. (Apple, Coca-Cola, Nike, Toyota) and Paul Bowen. Since graduating from Baylor University, Austin spent 7 months traveling to 19 countries on assignment to capture God's glory in photographs for missions organizations working all over the world. As well as shooting and editing photos, Austin is an accomplished graphic and web designer. "Photography has turned into something far more significant than a hobby or profession to me, it's become one of the very things that defines who I am; it's my creative outlet, an opportunity to bring out joy in other people and a chance to worship my God."

Please visit his excellent website: **www.austinmann.com**